# the other side of
# mulholland

Stephen Randall

# the other side of
# mulholland

**LA**
WEEKLY
BOOKS

*An LA Weekly Book for St. Martin's Press ≋ New York*

THE OTHER SIDE OF MULHOLLAND. Copyright © 2001 by Stephen
Randall. All rights reserved. Printed in the United States of
America. No part of this book may be used or reproduced in
any manner whatsoever without written permission except
in the case of brief quotations embodied in critical articles
or reviews. For information, address St. Martin's Press, 175
Fifth Avenue, New York, N.Y. 10010.

LA Weekly Books is a trademark of LA Weekly Media, Inc.

www.stmartins.com

Designed by Lorelle Graffeo

Library of Congress Cataloging-in-Publication Data

Randall, Stephen.
    The other side of Mulholland  /  Stephen Randall.
  —1st ed.
      p.   cm.
    ISBN 0-312-26216-7
    1.  Los Angeles (Calif.)—Fiction.   2.  Brothers—
Fiction.   3.  Success—Fiction.   I.  Title.

PS3618.A63 O8    2001
813'6—dc21

                                        2001020248

First Edition: June 2001

10  9  8  7  6  5  4  3  2  1

*For Gail and Nick*

*(without you, I'm toast)*

*Sometimes you're the windshield*

*Sometimes you're the bug*


**—Mark Knopfler**

# the other side of
# mulholland

# Like West Side Story, But with Sweat

**Like most gyms, the** 24-Hour Fitness on Pico contains two very distinct worlds, not to mention a caste system that makes India's seem laid-back. There's the Pump Room, with its free weights, its carefully sculpted bodies, its narcissistic, strutting muscle men who preen endlessly in the wall-to-wall mirrors and, operating under a new definition of heterosexuality that's as flexible as their bodies are hard, admire and touch one another, poking pecs, squeezing biceps, probing abs. They sweat, they strain, they work hard to look so perfect—and they enjoy the results a little too much. Thank you, *Men's Health,* for elevating vanity from one of the seven deadly sins to a virtue, like having clean fingernails and using deodorant.

Then there's the other area, the area so unimportant, it has no name. The men and women who work out in this area don't exercise nearly so hard nor look nearly so good. Apparently, there's only so much a Nautilus machine can do. But some of the machines have flashing lights, sound effects, and enough Nintendo touches so what you lack in muscle tone, you make up for by feeling contemporary. While the Pump Room is the domain of *guys* (with a few spectacular women who could never be as vain as the men, even though they deserve to be), the nameless room is the world of heart patients gamely following doctors' orders, grown-ups putting up a brave struggle against age, and young men who want to be in the Pump Room but can't quite carry it off.

Two worlds, like the Capulets and Montagues, the Sharks and Jets, USC and UCLA, UPN and PBS.

It was Friday morning at 9:00 and Perry, with a self-discipline that was positively Germanic, was in the Pump Room, studiously doing arm curls, looking in the mirror and watching that weird, prominent vein in his forehead pulsate like it was about to explode. He was up to three twelve-set reps of forty pounds, which wasn't bad for a twenty-six-year-old ectomorph. It was even more impressive, considering his hangover. Whatever possessed him to go drinking? The taping at *Boing!*—the cheesy cable game show kind enough to employ him as writer—couldn't have gone worse, with a series of questions so direly unfunny that Perry, already bleary-eyed and drained from the week, was forced to write more jokes in one hour than he had in the previous three weeks. At least they were good jokes, and the show had gotten done—albeit at 1:00 A.M., not 9:00 P.M. as scheduled. "You know," suggested Tom McMahon, the aged, campy host, who had parlayed his modest success as a disc jockey into a spiraling career of lesser and lesser game shows, "when I was on the network, the writers wrote funny stuff at the beginning and we didn't have to go through this shit at the last minute."

"Welcome to the wonderful world of cable," Perry had answered dryly.

"I'm serious," said McMahon. "If you don't change your attitude, this show will be never be on TVLand." Ah yes, thought Perry, the very definition of a classic—a show that ends up on TVLand, sometime after *Hogan's Heroes* but before *The White Shadow*. And with retro commercials. How cool!

"I want those residuals as much as anyone," Perry had said. Well, even more—since that was the whole point of anyone giving his life over to Hollywood—the same reason people robbed banks, for that matter. That's where the money was. He didn't bother to explain. He and two other writers had driven quickly to Barney's Beanery to get as drunk as possible as quickly as possible. Perry didn't much like Barney's Beanery—no one did, thanks to its manufactured seediness and boisterous clientele—but there were no other bars in that part of L.A. except gay bars. Getting seriously drunk had gone out of fashion west of La Brea Boulevard, and while that was a sizable inconvenience to a lot of drinkers, it was good news for Barney's.

Now, Perry had other problems than a surly star, a hangover, and a pulsating vein in his forehead. Tim was in the other area, the nameless area, rapidly bending over and over on some contraption that held out a vague promise of a flat stomach. Tim never looked in the wall-to-wall mirrors, because when he did, he saw a twenty-six-year-old who managed to be too fat and too skinny at the same time. He was so skinny, he drove the guy at Westime in the Westside Pavilion crazy, making him take so many links out of his new watchband that there was hardly any band left. And yet just inches north, past the elbow, the bicep (it seemed a stretch even calling it a bicep) was—well, it was soft, almost chubby. Perry could never understand why Tim didn't get his life together, and the two hadn't spoken in weeks. Perry hadn't written Tim off—he could never bring himself to do that—but he was taking a Tim break, one of many he'd treated himself to over the years.

Tim knew all too well that Perry was there. He saw him enter, quickly deduced that a hangover was the problem du jour, and watched from the nameless area as Perry began his workout. Tim hated Perry's dedication. They were so much alike in so many ways—it wasn't even that long ago when they'd regularly worn each other's clothes—and now Perry had gone and fixed himself, while Tim remained broken. Perry was a hunk; Tim was not. Perry was successful; Tim was still struggling. Perry was smart and cynical and a sellout. Tim was smart and cynical and lost.

Tim bided his time. He knew Perry well enough to gauge when he'd lapse into a semiconscious state and would be easily confused. He sneaked up as Perry was bent over and stood quietly behind him, making sure his reflection in the mirror would be the first thing that Perry would see.

Perry felt awful. Exercising in this condition didn't make him feel any better; it just made him dizzy and nauseous. He looked up in the mirror to see if he was as pale and clammy as he felt. A quick look at his reflection and he realized he was sicker than he thought. Although he felt like he was sitting on a bench, the mirror doesn't lie—and in the mirror, he was standing tall. And wearing a dumb T-shirt. He looked down at his own T-shirt—a perfectly hip Billabong. He looked up at his reflection, which was sporting a silly freebie from Barnes & Noble. He looked down. He looked up. He turned around.

"I hate when you do that," Perry said, glowering at his brother.

"I love it. It's one of the few benefits of having you as a twin," countered Tim.

Perry realized his Tim break was officially over.

"I was going to call you," he said, with a certain resignation. "Are you going to dinner at Mom and Dad's Sunday?"

"I guess so," said Tim. "My life hasn't been quite boring enough lately. That should help it."

"I was thinking of bringing Nancy, just so Dad will have someone to talk travel to," said Perry.

"And to feed Mom's grandkid fantasies," added Tim. "We can play count the hints and see how many times she brings it up."

"Remember, you're the one who can turn any family dinner into Armageddon. I'll even pay you a hundred dollars if you do."

"You'll have to do better than that," said Tim. "You're rich."

"I could offer you a million and you'd still be too gutless."

"Oh, good. A double-dog dare. Just like when we had bunk beds. Wanna play Legos?"

"I'd rather you wait for Thanksgiving or Christmas anyway," said Perry. "I think you should save it for a special holiday."

"No wonder you're such a semisuccessful TV hack," said Tim, not without affection. "Only in the wonderful world of TV does someone choose Christmas to blurt out, 'Hey, Mom, hey, Dad, I'm a homo.'"

"That's why TV is better than life," said Perry. "It's so much more entertaining."

## Dinner at Mom's: Break Out the Paper Plates and Koo Koo Roo

*There are so few* things in life that you can count on. That Paul Moyer will make several entertaining flubs nightly on the KNBC 11:00 P.M. newscast. That Steve Edwards will always get a job. That the *Los Angeles Times* will ferret out its worst writer and give her a regular column. That no decent Mexican restaurant in the city will ever get better than a *B* grade from the health department.

Tim had something else he could count on. This was, after all, Sunday, and that meant a family dinner at the grand Newman estate in Studio City in the San Fernando Valley. And what an estate it was—a late sixties tract home with recessed lighting in the ceiling, a den with a wet bar, bedrooms like a Ramada Inn, a kidney-shaped pool, and a built-in propane barbecue. He and Perry had grown up in that house, and it was no surprise that upon reaching what passes for adulthood, they had both escaped over the hill to the other side of Mulholland, an entire area code away from Mom and Dad.

Just as he knew it would, the phone rang around 4:00 P.M. "Hi, honey," said the chipper voice on the other end. It was Mom, the housewife turned real estate agent turned family counselor. "Do your dad and me a big favor, will you? Swing by the Koo Koo Roo on Ventura Boulevard on your way and pick up the chicken." Floating deep in the repressed mists of his childhood memories, he could recall images of his mother cooking. But that was before the big real estate boom of the eighties, when there were fortunes to be made matching up desperate buyers with small homes at exorbitant fees. Ann Newman hadn't exactly made a fortune, but she kept busy, and that—to all concerned—was the most important thing.

"Why do I always have to pick up dinner? How come Perry never has to?"

"He's bringing a date, dear," said Ann sensibly. "What type of impression would that make? I'll phone Koo Koo Roo and Daddy will pay you when you get here. You do have enough cash, don't you?"

"Sure, I can handle it," he said. He kept silent about the impression that having fast food for dinner might make, regardless of who picked it up. There were times when he positively admired his mother's selective vision. She'd been on a Koo Koo Roo chicken kick ever since the deep-voiced restaurant critic on talk radio intoned, "It's too good to be called fast food." Gossip columns reported how Bob Evans used Koo Koo Roo to cater screenings at his house and Lee Iacocca sat on Koo Koo Roo's board of directors. But that was before Evans had had his stroke and Iacocca had decided that there was more money to be made in marketing electric bicycles and the whole Koo Koo Roo mystique went to hell. As so often happens when things go to hell, word never reached the Valley.

No matter how often he or Perry complained that, as legitimate offspring making the long trek to Studio City, they deserved a home-cooked meal rather than fast food, Ann would look shocked. "Merrill Shindler on KLSX says it's too good to be called fast food," she'd say. That would be followed with a satisfied smile, the one that said, Nothing's too good for my family.

Of course, as fast food went, Koo Koo Roo was pretty good. And a bit pricey. Tim looked in his wallet. He didn't have anywhere near enough cash for dinner, unless they were all going to split a single marinated breast. Yet another meal would be financed at 21.7 percent APR.

Due to the long line at Koo Koo Roo and a minor dispute about Tim's maxed-out Visa card, which made him very glad he had a MasterCard fallback, Perry and Nancy were already ensconced in the den at casa Newman, drinking diet Coke while Syd, the patriarch of the Newman family, and Nancy discussed the merits of the Admiral's Club versus the Red Carpet Club.

"Neither one of them is worth the money," said Syd emphatically. A lifetime in car sales had given him the ability to sound completely sure of himself, even when he knew nothing. When it came to travel—his favorite subject of discussion—that was usually the case. Despite a bookcaseful of travel books, despite a daily flood of E-mail from Arthur Frommer and Travelzoo, despite a conversational repertoire that seemed limited to modes of transportation and hotels at various destinations, Syd traveled not at all. "Don't have time," he'd explain when either Tim or Perry pointed out the contradiction. "Maybe later."

Nancy, on the other hand, actually did travel. It came with

the job. She was the personal assistant to one of the most talked-about young actresses in Hollywood, one known for her numerous love affairs with some famous Gen-X actors and her exquisite taste in tattoos. Heather Windward and Nancy wandered the world together, particularly during those brooding post–love affair trips to Italy and France. They were close enough in age so that many people assumed employer and employee were friends. Nancy subtly fostered that delusion, not because she wanted to be a star's friend, but because it might help her get one of her projects off the ground and land the job of her dreams—that of producer. Not that she had any actual projects. With a limited budget, Nancy would be able to option only lesser books—say a murder mystery written by a self-educated retiree in Ohio and miraculously released as a quickie paperback. She could get a year's option on a book like that for two hundred dollars and shop it around. Instead, she took her two hundred and ordered embossed business cards. It gave her a feeling of satisfaction equaled only by the time her picture appeared next to her boss in *Us* magazine. She didn't get her name in the caption—it simply read ". . . and friend"—but she bought forty copies anyway, then mailed them to important people, carefully stapling a business card to each one. She didn't expect a response, but she labored mightily under the delusion that her minimailing had raised her profile.

Everyone took their diet Cokes to the table. "Oh, this is a special occasion," Perry commented, holding his plate aloft. "Mom broke out the good paper plates, the ones with plastic coating."

"Shut up, please," said Ann, thumping Perry with a plastic spoon.

There was a momentary silence, and unfortunately, Nancy chose to fill it.

"How's the job hunt coming, Tim?" she asked.

Oh, why? wondered Tim. Things had been going so well.

"I have a job interview tomorrow," he offered, "to do some writing for a Web site."

"A Web . . . site," said Ann, stretching out the words as if she were trying to dissect them. "A Web site. That sounds like it might be fun." She paused. "Is there much money writing for a Web site?"

Perry stepped in to save his brother. "Come on, Mom. It's what all of us will eventually be doing."

"Speaking of Web sites, have you seen Travelzoo?" asked Syd, inadvertently derailing the conversation and returning to the safe, boring world of travel. Tim was relieved.

There was ice cream and coffee (in actual cups!), and then the evening was over. Perry and Nancy, having arrived first, were able to duck out first. It was pretty much accepted in the family that any visit by Perry was a gift—after all, he had a job, a girlfriend, and spent more time at the gym. It showed how truly generous he was to spend any time with his family at all. Tim was not so lucky. Even on those rare occasions when he was busy, he didn't look it. So it fell on him to be the more dutiful son. On this particular night, he had a choice. Go back to his one-room apartment and watch *The Sopranos* by himself or stay with Mom and Dad and watch *The Sopranos* with them. He opted for company. When it was over, he kissed his mother and gave his dad a hug.

"I'll walk you to your car," said Syd.

As they approached the Honda Civic, Syd fished out his wallet. "I owe you for dinner," he said. "I almost forgot." He nervously, almost reluctantly, shoved two one-hundred-dollar bills in Tim's hand. "Take it—I don't have anything smaller."

"Dad." Tim sighed. "One one-hundred-dollar bill is smaller than two."

"Take it," insisted Syd. "And good luck tomorrow."

## Perry and Nancy Take the Plunge, Hollywood-Style

**Tim immediately noticed two** things about the offices that housed the *Hollywood Today* Web site staff. First, everything about it seemed temporary, as if the entire operation could move out overnight, leaving only a Sparketts cooler and some rented furniture. Second, everyone was either young or old—there was no one in between. The Dilbert-style cubicles were occupied by energetic twenty-somethings, bouncing around the office on a Mountain Dew high. But in the glass-encased offices with the nice views of ugly Culver City were the older guys—fifty plus, Tim figured. Maybe they were younger, but they looked so gray and beaten, it was hard to tell. He had seen something like this once before, when he took an ill-fated job as an associate editor on a small start-up magazine in West Hollywood. The staff consisted of two worlds—young up-and-comers, eager to make their mark, and older losers, editors who couldn't hack it at established magazines due to some personality flaw or substance-abuse problem. They had résumés, though, and seemed experienced, so they inevitably landed the good jobs at new magazines—until they were found out and sent on their way. Why should new media be any different from old media?

Simon James was old even for old media. But he was also well regarded. For nearly forty years, he had been one of those semifamous editors in New York, the number-two guy on a big magazine, the one who did all the work while his boss, who had a wardrobe allowance, attended all the parties. Writers loved Simon. Everyone loved Simon. He was so loved, in fact, that when he came up with a concept for his own magazine, a meglomaniacal Hollywood studio head had been more than happy to finance it out of his own pocket. So Simon moved west, published one issue of his dream magazine, and was promptly fired by the mogul, who appointed himself editor. The magazine died after the next issue, and Simon, too embarrassed to return to New York, began living a modest life with his severance package, and taking the occasional minor publishing job—the only kind that seemed to pop up in L.A. At the moment, for instance, he was running *Hollywood Today*, a Web site dedicated to covering the entertainment industry.

"I can't pay you very much," he told Tim after poring over his clips and asking a few extraordinarily perceptive questions. "We might have some fun, though. Do you want the job?" Tim didn't care much for *Hollywood Today*, but he was in awe of Simon James. He was also unemployed, broke, and bored. It was the easiest decision he'd ever made.

Tim waited until dinnertime before he called to tell his parents the good news. That way, they could each be on an extension and he'd only have to tell the story once. He prepared himself for their reaction. He'd been unemployed for too long, existing on freelance scraps and the odd extra hundred-dollar bill from Dad. He girded himself for an overly enthusiastic response from his mother, who had enough training in the disturbed sciences to understand—however slightly—the power of positive feedback.

"That's great news, Timmy," said his mother. "This has been such a wonderful day, what with your good news and your brother's good news. Syd, let's have everyone over for dinner Sunday to celebrate."

"Perry's good news?" Tim asked. "What's Perry's good news?"

Was it because they were twins? Was it something that affected all siblings? Was it the fact that his mother was partly crazy? Tim had always wondered why whenever one brother did something, it was always immediately linked to the other. Ann could seldom mention one without an instant comparison. "Perry loves golf, but Tim prefers watching TV." "We always count on Tim to program our VCR, but Perry knows the best restaurants." "Perry has a wonderful girlfriend, but Tim has always been a loner."

"Perry has some exciting news, too. I'm very proud of both my boys," chirped Ann.

"So am I supposed to guess about Perry's news? Or should I assume I'll read about it in the papers?" asked Tim.

"I wouldn't be surprised if you did," said Ann in a singsongy voice that made Tim's skin crawl.

"For God's sake, Ann, it's not that big," interjected Syd.

"It could be," insisted Ann.

"Oh, Jesus—he's not marrying Nancy, is he? How long have they been going out? Three months? He barely knows her."

"She's an extraordinary girl, Timothy. And she's very ambitious. She even reminds me a bit of myself. But no, to put your selfish mind at ease, they're not getting married. Yet."

"It's stupid," said Syd. "They're forming a production company together. It means nothing."

"You're so negative." Ann sighed. "You just wait until they have a hit series on the air. Besides, I think it would be fun to have your own production company."

Suddenly, no one seemed all that excited by Tim's news, not even Tim. He lingered on the phone line after the good-byes and his mother's final click. Thanks to his father's unrepaired deviated septum, he could hear breathing.

"Hi, Dad," he said.

"I realized I didn't congratulate you," said his father. "I'm sure this job will work out well."

"Thanks, Dad. You want your two hundred dollars back?"

"Keep it," said Syd after thinking a few seconds. "But you buy the Koo Koo Roo this Sunday."

They hung up, and Tim immediately called his brother.

"You make me sick," Tim said.

"Very funny. I take it you talked to Mom."

"So what's behind this new production deal? Since Don Simpson is dead, she's picked you?"

"You know Nancy. She thinks her real talent is producing."

"Repeat after me," said Tim. "Producing is not a talent. Producing is what the people with no talent do."

"My feelings exactly. That means she'll be perfect for it. But don't ever tell her I said that."

"Then why did you do it? Why does every straight couple in Los Angeles feel the necessity to form a production company? Gay couples don't do that."

"I look at it this way, Timmy boy. If I lived in Butte, Montana, and had a girlfriend, she'd want some way to cement the deal. She's probably make me buy a dog, and we'd consider it *our* dog. It would be a sign that we were a couple and were one step closer to marriage. Since this is L.A., I don't have to get a dog, which is great, since I can't handle the responsibility. Instead, I get a production company. It's certainly better than moving in together. I'm not ready for that. We're still getting to know each other."

"What is this production company going to do?"

"We're going to have stationery," said Perry, as if it was the most obvious thing in the world. "That's the key attraction. It will take Nancy a month to get the stationery she wants. Meanwhile, even shopping for stationery will make her happy, and Mom's happy because she thinks I'm one step closer to marriage."

"If Mom only knew the real you, then I could be the favorite," said Tim, laughing. "You know that, don't you?"

"You're just jealous. Admit it—you're a sad, petty little man who lives in my shadow," said Perry with mock superiority. "You're just thinking, Poor me, I don't even have anybody to form a production company with. I'll go through my whole life without stationery."

"I'd rather have a dog, thank you very much," said Tim. "And now that I have a job, I might be able to afford one."

"A job? A real job? My, my, aren't we the competitive one."

"I got my job this morning," countered Tim. "When did the megamerger take place?"

"Lunch—at Pane e Vino," answered Perry. "You win."

Tim filled Perry in on the new job—about Simon James and the odd mix of very young and very old at *Hollywood Today*. There were good things about having a writer as a brother. At least he knew the cast of characters and understood the game. There were bad things, too, and they were painfully obvious, all involving potent sibling rivalry that never seemed to dissipate.

As the conversation wound down, Perry's mind wandered

a bit. "So Mom was really impressed by the production company, huh?" he asked.

"Yes." Tim sighed. "She really was."

"She doesn't have a clue, does she?"

"Not the slightest," said Tim.

# Ann Leans Toward Separation and Syd Is Glad

**It was a couple** of years earlier that Ann had first noticed a most disturbing trend. First, it was one or two couples. Then four or five, which was a lot. What with all the demands on her time, Ann could never juggle more than six or seven couples a week as it was. Those couples all came to see her with a creepy alien goal in mind: How can we save our marriage? They were sincere about it, too. It was a given in Ann's industry that anytime a couple entered therapy, one was looking for an easy exit, or maybe both. Ann wasn't a marriage counselor. Like the others, she was a divorce facilitator. But that was changing. The good old days when couples went to a family counselor to break free of each other—consequences be damned—were beginning to wane, and Ann wasn't happy about it. You don't need to have a Ph.D.—and, of course, Ann didn't—to figure out that people wanting to stay married bodes ill for those in the marriage-counseling business. If marriage made a comeback, and people decided to stick by each other even during the tough times, soon they wouldn't bother seeking counseling at all. It's that damn Hillary Clinton's fault, thought Ann. Stand by your man, indeed!

Ann had been through this once before, with her first post-motherhood career as a real estate agent. For a while during the eighties, real estate money was like Starbucks coffee—you couldn't escape it. Not that Ann became rich. After all, she was a mother and a wife and a friend and a shopper, and she took those roles seriously. However, she rather enjoyed the peaceful Sundays at open houses, and doing the Sunday crossword puzzle, schmoozing with the occasional prospect while sitting in the sunny dining room of a house not her own. Sadly, trends die, and housing prices leveled off. People, unable to make a quick fortune by selling, stayed put. Ann was disappointed but undaunted, and she immediately enrolled in a special course at Antioch College in Marina del Rey to become a counselor. She loved the challenge, but what she loved best was the fact that Antioch gave her life credits simply for being a wife and mother, cutting her studies down by a full year. Syd and the boys scoffed and called it "a diploma mill," but to Ann, it merely showed how imminently sensible Antioch was.

Now it was time for another career change. Ann retired to her backyard to think and drink her early-morning coffee. Syd sat in the breakfast nook, pretending to read Emeril Lagasse's new cookbook but secretly watching his wife, wondering what her next career might be. He knew she needed to have a career, and that that career needed to be extremely flexible. Even with the boys grown, Ann wasn't about to sacrifice her outside interests—like lunch at Pinot Bistro and sales at the Sherman

Oaks Fashion Square and her book club. But with the problems at his car dealership—problems he couldn't bring himself to share with anyone in the family—he hoped it was a low-overhead career. Her stint as a marriage counselor had been a fiscal flop. Ann kept the checks from her handful of clients, but Syd paid the exorbitant rent on her office and had financed Antioch, all without complaint.

Ann thought about what was important to her; her family, her home, her neighborhood. She pondered the things that threatened what she loved: earthquakes, gang members, bad schools, the general deterioration of the world around her. She couldn't help but think back to the days when the boys were young, when public schools were plenty good enough, when Du-Par's, Studio City's favorite old-fashioned coffee shop, wasn't haunted by dirty homeless men with their palms outstretched. Life was nicer then, and Ann—truth be told—was happier. What type of career would allow her to turn back the clock?

Then it hit her. She marched into the kitchen and faced Syd.

"I'm closing my practice," she announced. "I've found something else I need to do."

Syd looked up quizzically. "I'm all ears," is what he said, but what he was thinking was, Shit, I have another seven months on the lease on her goddamn office!

"I can't just sit around and do nothing, Syd. You know that's not my style." Syd nodded insincerely. "And I just don't feel I can make a difference dealing with all these troubled couples and their same old problems. I know you don't take my job all that seriously, Syd, but it's hard. I deal with a lot of negativity. It takes a toll, even on a strong person like me."

"I'm sure it does. And I think you're holding up very well."

Ann either ignored that comment or simply didn't hear it. Syd could never tell.

"So I asked myself, How can I make the best use of my talents? And then it hit me."

"Go on."

"It dawned on me that everything bad in life comes from *over there,* and it all comes straight over Laurel Canyon," she said, pointing in the general vicinity of evil Los Angeles. "I want to keep all those terrible things on that side of the hill, where they belong."

"You're building a guard station?" he asked. "Putting spikes in the road at Mulholland?"

"I'm going to volunteer to help with the secession movement, to help make the Valley its own city," she said with pride. "I think I can make a difference."

Among the general weirdness to come from California—Jerry Brown, cell phones, and that whole bottled water thing—Valley secession ranked very high. Critics liked to complain that it was racially motivated, and while true, it didn't begin to hint at the basic cause. The Valley had an inferiority complex bigger than David Geffen's expense account. When L.A. proper was a young sapling of a metropolis, the Valley was full of orange groves. As the city grew and prospered, the Valley became the bedroom community for people not quite successful enough to live in *real* Los Angeles. Even as L.A. began its decline into seediness, the valley still lost the PR war—dismissed as a vast expanse of tract homes, lighting-fixture stores, and Jiffy Lubes. Like Australia, with its illustrious history as a penal colony, the Valley would never be fully accepted as part of the empire. That hurt more than the lingering fear that the blacks would someday escape South Central and set up shop detailing cars in Reseda.

To politicians, secession threatened to kill a semigreat city.

But for Syd, it was an opportunity. He did some quick head math. Ann's lack of income would be easily matched by the lack of expenses, especially if he could sublet her office. Volunteer work was clearly the most profitable career she had ever considered.

"I think that's wonderful, dear," he said. As Ann went to call her friends to tell them the news, Syd returned to his cookbook. He loved his cookbooks almost as much as his travel books. Of course, he never cooked, either.

# Simon James Cuts the Cheese

**Had Tim been straight,** he could have easily fallen in love with the girl in the next cubicle. He had been working at *Hollywood Today* for less than a week, and Sandy had already emerged as the one true character in the office. Pretty, but in a cute way, with wispy hair that seemed unusually affected by the slightest static electricity or weakest air currents, Sandy was the resident daffy genius—you could never be sure whether she had stumbled into some of the funny things she said, or whether she was just that clever. She was a lovable curmudgeon, if such a thing is possible, and she got away with sarcastic comments that would have ruined other friendships, but which merely seemed funny coming from such an habitually confused face. A bright, witty writer—at least when you read her finished copy—she seemed to know very little about show business and got easily baffled by the few facts she did know.

Her head popped up over the partition with alarming regularity and even more alarming questions.

"Is Walter Cronkite dead or alive?" she asked, poking her head up. The prevailing winds in the office must have been blowing east, since her hair pointed left.

"Alive," answered Tim.

She eyed him quizzically. "Are you sure?" she asked slowly.

"Very old but very alive," said Tim, but he could tell Sandy was not fully convinced. "Like Abe Vigoda."

"Who's Abe Vigoda?" she asked.

Five minutes passed. "Marilyn Manson and RuPaul—which one is the real woman?" she asked. The nonexistent breeze had shifted and her hair now tilted right.

"Please tell me you're joking." Tim laughed. "You're an entertainment reporter, not a grandmother. They're both men. Everyone knows that."

"I thought there might be a trick in this one," she said with a sigh, and sat back down. Before this job, Sandy had never seen *Entertainment Tonight*, let alone *Variety*. She might as well have taken a job at ESPN, considering her lack of knowledge.

Before she could ask another question, Simon James appeared at Tim's cube. He was the only man in the entire office to wear a suit, an old tweedy suit that smelled of cigarettes. "Sandy, this involves you, too," he said, and Sandy's head quickly sprang over the partition, hair wafting toward the rear.

"I've been meaning to take you both to lunch to get to know you better, and I thought today might be a good day, unless one of you has other plans." No one admits to other plans when the boss comes calling, so they agreed to meet at Simon's office at 12:30 P.M.

Real estate was cheap in Culver City, where *Hollywood Today* had its offices. Of all the cities on the Westside, Culver City was the most out of place, a dowdy little town that belonged farther inland, away from even a hint of glamour. It was poorer than any of its neighbors and managed to keep many of the vestiges of a small town. Even the massive presence of Sony Pictures couldn't seem to draw a decent restaurant to the area. But it had a Main Street—a real main street, almost like Disneyland's—with a hardware store, a beauty college, and parking meters that still took pennies. Main Street also had Novacento, a funky Italian restaurant with good food that existed under the radar. It never made Zagat's or any restaurant reviews, but it still managed to exist handsomely on hungry Sony execs and people from the neighborhood.

"Let me give you some advice," said Simon as they sat down. "Be careful of the first person who tries to be your friend at any new job. That's almost always the person who's alienated everyone else and is desperate for new blood." Neither Tim nor Sandy could figure out whom he was warning them about—no one talked much to either of them.

But Simon flowed with advice—and praise. He told them how impressed he'd been with their early work, and how, after forty years as an editor, he was fairly convinced that he'd developed a certain sense for talent and that they both had it.

As he talked, it seemed as if no aspect of their lives was off-limits. Simon knew books they should read, movies they should see, countries they should visit. It wasn't obnoxious at all—in fact, Tim wanted to blurt out, Will you adopt me? because Simon was such a natural father figure. Better yet, he was a dad with a lot of experience, who seemed to have taken a liking to his two new charges.

Tim's pasta and scampi arrived. "Would you like cheese with that?" asked the waiter.

Simon held out his hand. "Never put Parmesan on seafood," he warned, as if the combo might be combustible. "No gourmet ever does. It makes it too salty."

Tim made a mental note. So did Sandy, who picked at a spinach salad but figured she had gleaned yet another useful nugget from her new boss.

Three bites into his lunch, Tim felt a presence behind him.

Sandy, who was sitting opposite him, got a confused look on her face. "I think I'm seeing double," she said.

Tim turned around and found Perry and Nancy standing behind him, smiling. Their fledgling production company, Comstock Productions, had just taken its first meeting at Columbia TriStar on the Sony lot, pitching a TV series, and both were giddy. No promises had been made, but the meeting seemed to have gone very well, and the happy partners had just finished lunch at a nearby table. Introductions were made, and Nancy produced fancy new business cards with a flourish. No one else even tried to compete.

"We told them what our company was trying to do, and they respected that," said Nancy, and even Perry had to roll his eyes. But pragmatic Perry was still optimistic. "We pitched to one guy, and within thirty minutes we were pitching again to three biggies," he said. "Plus, they asked us not to talk to anyone else until they could talk it over."

"I might call Fox anyway," said Nancy. "It's not like anyone wrote us a check."

"I think we can give them a few days to think about it," maintained Perry firmly. Now it was Nancy's turn to roll her eyes.

Later, back at the office, Sandy's head popped up. "Would you read my copy?" she asked.

Tim blanched. "Sure," he said, clicking on Sandy's folder on his screen. It was only 450 words, but they were 450 attitude-laden words, which were great fun to read. Even more impressive, they seemed to be written by someone who knew what she was talking about.

"I have a question," asked Tim as Sandy's head reappeared. "Are you an idiot savant?"

"You know," said Sandy thoughtfully, "you're not the first person to ask me that."

"It's very good. Very funny," said Tim.

"Oh, thank you," said Sandy, clearly relieved. "Now I have something else I want to ask you."

"I'm listening."

"How come if you're the gay one, your brother has all the nice clothes?"

Tim laughed out loud. In part, it was an involuntary reflex to being outed—he had been careful not to say anything that would have given a hint of his sexual orientation. And he laughed because it was true. He was a fashion failure, while Perry—under Nancy's tutelage—looked great.

"What can I tell you?" Tim stammered. "I don't like show tunes, either. I'm not a very good homosexual."

"I can fix that," said Sandy. "Tomorrow at lunch, I'm taking you shopping. I'll fix you. I could tell your brother was sort of a jerk, and you can't go around having him look better."

"He's only a jerk about show business," protested Tim.

"He's a jerk if he's involved with that girl," said Sandy.

"And a jerk about Nancy," he admitted. "But she has nice business cards."

"And this time tomorrow, you'll have nice clothes. It'll cost you an entire paycheck, but it'll be worth it."

"How about a partial fixing?" said Tim, thinking dollars and cents.

"Okay, part this week and part when you get your next paycheck. Then we'll move on."

"What do you mean, 'move on'?"

"You know, the works. We start with some clothes, then move on to your hair. Think of it as Sandy Moore Life-Management Services. We take care of everything. Eventually, I'll even choose all new friends for you. But first, we shop. We style. We find you a gym."

"I already belong to a gym," said an indignant Tim.

Sandy's face scrunched up into its most bewildered look yet as she carefully eyed Tim from top to bottom.

"You've got to be kidding," she said.

# The Curse of the Twelve-Steppers

**It was only 10:00 A.M.,** and already Nancy felt the need for a Kava Kava. She paced around the guest house that served as her office, wearing her cordless headset, cursing the mere existence of twelve-step programs. As far as Nancy could tell, messenger services only hired recent graduates from AA or NA or some other A, and, professionally speaking, this left much to be desired. It explained why she was now on the phone with her third messenger service in the past ten minutes, trying to find one that could actually get its act together enough to pick up a script at Fox, a mere half hour from Heather's home in Laurel Canyon, and deliver it promptly to the house. Of course, for Nancy—and for Heather—*promptly* meant "right now," certainly within the hour. However, when you're taking life one day at a time, the way most messengers do, *promptly* has a more flexible definition.

Nancy walked outside to the pool, which stretched the range of her cordless headset to the max. "Is noon okay?" she asked Heather, who sat fully clothed poolside, her brooding demeanor and black outfit a stark contrast to the cheerfully sunny day and clear blue sky. She took small sips of iced tea to offset the dry mouth caused by her new prescription of Celexa.

Heather didn't answer. She simply tightened her grip on her iced tea and grimaced. It's all too much, she thought to herself. It isn't even worth it.

Her displeasure noted, Nancy shifted into gear. "Two hours is unacceptable," she said sternly. "Do you know who we're talking about? Do you realize what's a stake here? If you can't get that script here in one hour, not only will we never use you again but I can assure you that once word gets out, no one will want to use you." Her voice lifted to a bit of a shout. "Do you understand what I'm saying?"

Of course, the man on the other end of the phone knew exactly what she was saying. He'd heard it before. He'd heard it from the caller before Nancy and he knew he'd hear it from his next call, as well. Scripts needed to move quickly around town. If you weren't the first to get it, well, what was the point? He guaranteed one-hour service, knowing full well that it would take two. This way, everyone was happy—at least for the moment.

Nancy stuck her head out toward the pool. "It'll be here in forty-five minutes," she said confidently. "No problem."

"Why is it so hard?" asked Heather wistfully.

"What can I say? Messenger services suck," answered Nancy.

"That's not what I meant," said Heather. She looked away, which Nancy took as a sign to close the door of the guest house and give Heather her space.

Nancy pressed Perry's speed call. "You know what would make us rich?" asked Nancy. "A really good messenger service, one that can actually deliver on time. Everyone would use it."

Perry pondered Nancy's latest scheme for a brief second. "Nah," he said. "Do you know what those guys smell like? I have to ride in the elevator with them, so I know. It wouldn't be worth it."

"So we'd hire clean messengers. It would make people even more likely to use us. No one wants things delivered by a smelly messenger."

Perry sighed. "I'll get on it Tuesday," he said. That's what he always said when he wanted to switch topics away from one of Nancy's brainstorms. Since she forgot about things by dinner, it usually worked.

"I'm not joking," she said. "You think about it."

"I have better things to think about," Perry reminded her. "Like the series." The pitch meeting had gone well, and now Comstock Productions, Nancy and Perry's own little embryonic Carsey-Werner, was moving up to the next level. Words on paper. In the entertainment industry, putting words on paper was a significant step. Writers didn't much like it, because it meant actual work, and often, words on paper were more revealing than the glib pitchspeak that dominated most meetings. Studio execs agreed to it reluctantly, since they hated reading, and having a paper trail took away the convenience of deniability. Even in Hollywood, no one was quite comfortable committing several million dollars of some conglomerate's money without having at least a dozen pages of neatly typed text before them. Words on paper showed that everyone was making a best effort.

"You'll have words for me tonight," said Nancy. "Tonight's a good night for me to give you notes."

That was the division of labor at Comstock Productions. Nancy was the dynamo, the can-do girl. She harassed executives into meeting with them with a fervor that almost frightened the more passive Perry. He was the creative one, the workhorse. The sitcom for Columbia TriStar was his idea, but Nancy had gotten them to listen and had, to be sure, offered a few helpful suggestions. Now—in between writing wacky questions for *Boing!*—Perry was pounding out the treatment for their sitcom, the project that would lift him from the showbiz basement of cable to the penthouse of network TV without having to wander in the netherworld of syndication on the way. It made him love Nancy all the more.

And Nancy loved Perry. He was a good team player, and that was important. Nancy herself was a good team player—she knew that as she looked at her list of projects for the day: "Get Fox script; see if 29 Palms has room 201 available for Memorial Day weekend (but don't make reservations); set up hair appointment (but only after the shop has closed and Heather can have Yuki all to herself—you know what happened last time his mind wandered); find out if a new Ford Excursion can fit in Heather's driveway—if so, arrange test drive." But Nancy knew she could also be much more. That's what made Comstock Productions such a natural enterprise and Perry and Nancy such a wonderful team.

Heather stood at the door of the guest house. She was happier now, almost buoyant. "I'm going shopping at Fred Segal's," she said. "Call me on the cell if anything comes up."

"What about the script?" asked Nancy.

"I'm not really in the mood," said Heather. "Maybe tomorrow."

## "Are You Structure or Are You Gap?"

**Spring in Los Angeles** can be harsh. With temperatures occasionally dipping into the low seventies, it was easy to understand how Sandy, seemingly the picture of health on one day, could be laid low with a severe head cold the next. Tim didn't know she had a cold when she wandered into the office significantly late. He thought she had gotten lost. With her knit cap, wool scarf, winter coat, and gloves (gloves!), he simply assumed she was headed for Anchorage but had accidentally shown up at work instead.

"I dressed like that once," he told her. "But it was only because everything else I owned was dirty. What's your excuse?"

"I have a cold," said Sandy, as if Tim had once again missed something painfully obvious. "And we're supposed to go shopping during lunch today. Have you forgotten?"

"Nope—credit cards and checkbook are right here. We are going shopping in Los Angeles, I hope. I didn't bring any ski wear."

"You are very ungrateful. I'm taking you to Century City because it has the best clothes. I could take you to the West-side Pavilion, but I think too highly of you. And since we're going to Century City and I have a cold, I dressed accordingly."

"Those malls are maybe one mile apart," said Tim. "They're even in the same area code."

"Century City is an *outdoor* mall, stupidhead," said Sandy. "And you'll have to drive, because I took NyQuil by mistake this morning."

On a classically warm L.A. day, being outdoors was part of Century City's appeal. By the time Tim and Sandy arrived, the mall was swarming with office workers, racing to be first in line at the various classy fast-food restaurants so, in turn, they could get a nice outdoor table and not be forced to wander the food court with their lunch on a tray, lunging for a table the second it was vacant, eating their Tacone wraps amid a sea of Stage Deli litter.

Pizza by the slice is conveniently precooked, and thus terrifically efficient for the time-pressed shopper. There they sat—Sandy as if she were braving an arctic blast, and Tim, in jeans and a T-shirt, as if he was ready to paint the garage—surrounded by business uniforms: the women dressed as casually as the bank or law firm would allow (which was not very) and the men in suits, with the suit jackets still hanging on the back of their office doors and their ties tossed over their shoulders to avoid unsightly spills.

"I've never been a guy in a suit," said Tim, surveying his surroundings. "I wonder if I ever will be."

Sandy was pulling pills from a plastic container in her purse and arranging them in a line on her tray—two one-thousand-milligram vitamin C tablets, one echinacea and goldenseal, and two zinc lozenges. "You will never be a guy in a suit," she said with a certain authority. "How old are you?"

"Twenty-six."

"There'd be some sign of it by now, and believe me, there's none. Your brother, on the other hand, I can see him ending up as a guy in a suit."

"This is based on meeting him for three minutes?"

"You can tell these things," said Sandy. "It's not hard."

After they dumped their trays, the duo headed off for Tim's makeover. "Are you Structure or are you Gap?" asked Sandy.

"Right now, I'm Old Navy."

"That's a good start. We'll go to the Gap. When you get older, you can move up to Structure. That way, you'll have something to look forward to."

"You know what this reminds me of?" said Tim as they wandered from store to store, comparing the Gap with Banana Republic with J. Crew with Structure with Ambercrombie & Fitch. "It's like eating at a hotel. You have the coffee shop at one end and the nice restaurant at the other, but you just know all the food comes out of the same kitchen. These guys are just changing labels on us. I've seen the same cargo pants five times at five different prices."

They lingered for a moment outside Restoration Hardware. "When Sandy Moore Life-Management Services graduates to fixing my apartment, can I buy my furniture here?" he asked.

Sandy shook her head. "Too good for the likes of you. You're still in the Pier One phase. I'll bet you still have your TV on a cinder-block bookcase."

"The world is much too hard on cinder-block bookcases," complained Tim. "You'd be surprised how well they withstood the earthquake."

"If you're very good, I'll let you look in Pottery Barn or

Crate & Barrel. But no Restoration Hardware until you get a big raise. Anyway, your hair comes next. Where do you get it cut?"

"One of those strip mall places. Fantastic Sam's, or whatever doesn't have a line."

"You're making this extra-challenging, aren't you?" said Sandy disapprovingly.

A stunning $475 later, Tim had new clothes. Not drastically different clothes, but enough of an improvement to make him feel as if they were *his* clothes and he was not some fashion imposter.

"Thanks," he said as he loaded the clothes into his trunk. "I would have never done this on my own."

"It was fun," said Sandy, blowing her nose. "Dressed properly, you're almost a good-looking guy. It's too bad you're gay."

# Nancy Writes a Memo to Perry

*Dear Perry:*

*I think this is absolutely the most wonderful thing you've ever written. There's no way that Columbia TriStar won't snap this up in a second. It's funny, it's warm, and I can see it running for years on network and then on into even more profitable eternity in syndication. You are a genius.*

*I have such passion for this project. I know you do, too, and I know that soon Columbia will share our passion.*

*Sometimes I'm so in awe of your talent. I might know how to run things and make things happen, but you can create. It makes me jealous. I know how lucky I am to be listed as cocreator with you.*

*When we make the official presentation to Columbia, I hope you don't overshadow me at the meeting. They'll love what we've done so much, they'll be falling all over themselves at your feet. Let me do some of the talking— anyway, we both know that talking is one of the things that I do best.*

*Since the meeting is tomorrow afternoon, why don't I just meet you at the studio? There's no reason for you to come all the way to Laurel Canyon to get me. I showed your treatment to Heather and she loves it and is full of wonderful casting ideas. (Imagine Sean Patrick Flannery as the brother. Is that perfect or what?) Even though she keeps telling me that she hates the idea of losing me, she's pulling for us. She's going to call Jonathan at Columbia to put in a good word. Isn't that sweet? And she wants me to call her the minute the meeting is over. We've spent hours talking about this. It's made us much closer.*

*I'll meet you in the east parking lot about fifteen minutes before. You might want to wear your dark green pants from Banana Republic and the cream Ambercrombie & Fitch shirt with that tie your mom gave you. Don't wear a jacket—you'll look too old. Your white Nikes are fine, and be sure to gel your hair the way I showed you, not that other way, which looks dorky.*

*See you tomorrow.*

*Love and kisses,*

*Nancy*

**My girlfriend actually writes** me memos, thought Perry. Not notes. Memos. Maybe they're love memos, a new form of communication. And she tells me where to park and what to wear. That's me—Project Perry. Will she ever be done improving me? he wondered. And what will happen then?

Perry had his own method of self-improvement. It involved a surreptitious visit to the beauty-supply story at the mall, often done best during midday on a quiet weekday like today, when he was least likely to run into someone he knew. It wasn't so much that he was patronizing a beauty-supply store that embarrassed him—that seemed pretty normal among his group of friends and coworkers. It was what he bought. Even the sales staff eyed him suspiciously, and he was self-conscious enough to always pay cash, rather than reveal his name.

If you asked Tim, he could easily dismiss his twin brother as vain—the nice clothes, the rigorous workouts, the meticulously gelled hair. Even Tim barely realized how deep Perry's vanity ran, especially when it came to hair. Hair was Perry's secret obsession. It made sense in a way. He had a thick mop of dark hair—thick even for a twenty-six-year-old—and people often commented on it. It was darker and thicker than Tim's, and Tim's was plenty thick enough. Even Syd had a good solid head of hair for a sixty-year-old. But Tim and Syd took their hair for granted, and Perry did not. He loved his hair. It was a mane of honor, and Perry intended to keep it that way, despite considerable expense.

The expense involved Nioxin, a grotesquely overpriced line of hair-care products for balding men. There was the special shampoo, full of bionutrients to encourage healthy hair growth. There was Scalp Therapy, a fancy botanical conditioner he let sit on his head for a full five minutes every morning. The most potent weapon in his hair self-defense arsenal was the Bionutrient Treatment, a spray with a long, ominous nozzle that saturated his scalp. He allowed that to work its magic for a full minute every morning, despite the fact that it turned his scalp bright red and caused big red blotches when it dripped on his face or chest. The blotches lasted only a few minutes, and Perry was happy to see them, viewing them as empirical proof that this stuff actually did *something*.

Add in Nioxin Structure and Strength (a triple-bonding reconstructor for damaged hair) and Nio Gel (the weightless styling gel), and Perry had run up a tab of another two hundred dollars in hair-care products. The Korean woman bagged his purchases and shook her head.

"You no need this," she said in broken English, handing him the bag.

There wasn't much Perry could say. He smiled and hurried from the store.

## Upper Los Angeles and Lower Los Angeles Made Easy

**For reasons Tim didn't** fully understand, the journalism teacher at Pepperdine had thoughtfully provided a class roster for Journalism 435, aka "Advanced Emerging Media," aka, "How you can make a living on the Web if you don't get a real journalism job." The roster featured a polyglot of names, several with letters not of our alphabet, making the list look a little like the periodic table of elements. But what seemed multicultural on paper was downright white-bread in the flesh. A roomful of very blond, very tan, very Christian cheerleaders and surfers stared blankly at Simon James, who was the featured star, a guest lecturer talking about his good old days in New York with Breslin and Talese to a group of students who got their news from Pat Robertson's 700 Club. Tim felt positively ethnic. In Los Angeles, it's easy to forget you're Jewish, especially if you'd been brought up in an ambivalently atheist household that didn't even attend, let alone take part in, bar mitzvahs and the like. "We're delicatessen, not synagogue," Syd liked to say. Even when you remember, you're surrounded by other Jews, often more Jewishy Jews, so you hardly feel out of place. At Pepperdine, a wealthy Christian college with the world's most blessed location—across the street from the beach in Malibu—he felt like Timmy the Ape Boy: older, shorter, fatter, and swarthier. Even Perry would be intimidated by this group, thought Tim. Simon had asked Tim to come along for moral support, but Tim had to wonder if the lanky, patrician Simon had wanted to bring along a darker counterpart just so that he might seem even Waspier by comparison.

Although girls outnumbered the boys by two to one, as they do in all journalism classes, the boys asked all the questions. And all the questions centered on money. Their voices had that certain catch, as if just now, with graduation clearly on the horizon, they realized they had signed up for a low-paying profession and weren't too sure they liked the idea.

Simon managed both to reassure and depress them with his answers. "Yes, entry-level salaries are low. In fact, so are the top-level salaries. But that's just compared to high-paying professions, like law or business or medicine," said Simon. "You'll make more money than a teacher," he added, only to make the professor drop his head uncomfortably. "And there's always the chance of hitting the big score." Simon rattled off the names of writers who had seen their articles metamorphose into books or movies and reaped the mother lode as a result. "Does your garden-variety dermatologist stand a chance of getting one of those big paydays?" asked Simon. "Is he going to be on *Charlie Rose*?"

"I'm not a rich man," said Simon somewhat wistfully. "I

came close, but I never had one of my projects make me rich. It's probably too late for me now. But I can't say that I'd do anything any differently. You'll meet a lot of unhappy rich people in the world, and I'd rather be a happy journalist."

For a humble but happy journalist, Simon certainly has lavish tastes, thought Tim as he climbed into Simon's brand-new Lincoln Town Car for the ride back to Culver City. There's this car, the fancy lunches and dinners, all at company expense, the membership at Riviera Country Club, the large house in Benedict Canyon. Simon came across very much like a well-heeled lawyer, and Tim couldn't quite find the smoke and mirrors that made it work.

"Do you ever wish you had gone into another line of work?" asked Tim as they swooshed down Pacific Coast Highway.

"Like what?" replied Simon. "Movies? I had my close encounter with the movie business when the studio decided to bankroll my magazine. The lying. The hypocrisy. The idea of making a decision that affects dozens of lives and millions of dollars on a whim, without thinking things through. It nearly ruined my life. I couldn't become one of them."

"I'm surprised that you stayed in L.A."

"I didn't plan to," Simon continued. "It just sort of happened. You were born here, so you might not appreciate it as much. But you'll notice that while lots of people come to L.A. in search of something wonderful—just like I did—not that many find it, and that would include me. Yet they never go home. They get other jobs, they get married, they have kids, and they buy a house. They stay."

"If they don't make it here—I mean, find stardom or whatever brought them here in the first place—why do so many stay?"

"You've got to remember that there are two separate Los Angeleses. You probably know it and don't even realize it.

Think of L.A. as an iceberg. There's that tip that everyone can see. That's Hollywood, and all the glitz and the big houses and beautiful women and the BMWs. Upper Los Angeles. The mythologized Los Angeles. That's the L.A. you and I write about."

"Like the stars and Spago and the studios," interjected Tim.

"They're all there, in all their public glory. Everyone comes out to be part of upper Los Angeles. A few make it and get to live that life. I don't really envy them."

"And lower L.A.?"

"You probably grew up in lower Los Angeles. That's the better part."

"The Valley? That's the *better* part?"

"It's not geographic. It's more psychographic. It's the part of Los Angeles that's too dull to be the subject of a TV show or Joan Didion novel. It's normal life. It's people who came out here to be Cameron Diaz or Brad Pitt and ended up working for Allstate instead. At first, they're disappointed, but you can adjust to almost any reality. Pretty soon, you realize that lower Los Angeles is just like where you came from—families, homes, small businesses—but with better weather and less of those East Coast affectations or that midwestern stuffiness. It doesn't much matter what school you went to out here, or who your family is—you get to invent yourself. Or reinvent, if your first attempt fizzles. That's a good thing. That's why people stay. It's not stifling. You can grow."

"My family is definitely lower Los Angeles," said Tim. "Very lower."

"I'll bet your father has never even worked in the entertainment industry and couldn't care less about it."

"That's totally true," said Tim. "He has a car dealership in the Valley. A Honda dealership."

"Really? A car dealership," Simon was interested. "Does he own it?"

"He's the general manager of a partnership that owns it," explained Tim. "I don't have firm grip on the details—he's been doing it since I was kid and doesn't talk that much about it. He's done well, though."

"How does a partnership like that work?" asked Simon, who had pushed upper and lower Los Angeles out of his mind as they passed Topanga Beach and began to focus with surprising intensity on the ins and outs of retail auto sales. Tim couldn't tell if his boss was just being polite in giving him a turn to talk or if, like so many journalists, Simon James was congenitally, excessively curious and couldn't help himself.

## "Bring Me a Sheet of Clean White Paper!"

**Syd sat alone in** his darkened office at Newman's Super Honda, protected from the outside world by Gladys, the dealership's ferocious receptionist and his unofficial secretary. Unlike the rest of the car dealership, which was furnished in that impersonal prefab car dealership decor, Syd's office was plush and warm, with a big oak desk, a gigantic leather chair, and deep carpeting. He had a computer, a stereo, and a TV, but very few office supplies. Years ago, he had embarrassed himself in midmeeting when he was unable to jot down a phone number. "Gladys," he bellowed. "Bring me a sheet of clean white paper."

Gladys scurried in, placing one blank sheet of typing paper squarely on his empty desk. With a certain flourish, she also offered him a pen. To Gladys' credit, she was able to do both with a straight face.

Syd was not so lucky after the meeting. By that time, Gladys had told the story to everyone on the property and even to Ann, who had called during the meeting. "Bring me a sheet of clean white paper" became one of those moments that haunts a man, a standing joke that even Syd told on himself time and time again.

He could hear voices outside, salesmen, the service manager, all asking to speak to him, and he heard Gladys firmly turn them away, claiming he was busy. He was busy, or at least deep in thought. He fumbled with notes he had taken at his lunch meeting earlier. His partners were unhappy and he wasn't sure what he could do about it. For over twenty years, he'd been able to do something beyond sell cars—he'd been able to convince guys with money that owning part of a car dealership was a good investment. However, in an Amazon.com–type world, a nice steady return on your money no longer seemed good enough. His partners were itchy—they didn't know where they wanted to put their cash, but they were damn well sure that there had to be something sexier and more lucrative than selling Civics and Accords.

This depressed Syd. Or maybe it didn't. Syd could never quite tell if he was depressed or not. He often turned to his wife, who, after all, had some training in these matters, to tell him. Sometimes she surprised him. "I think you're very depressed," she'd say, often when he felt merely calm. Or: "I've never seen you so happy," when Syd was in the midst of a major anxiety attack.

Mostly, though, she got it right. And she'd been getting it right long before she had any professional schooling in various mood disorders. "I know you better than you know yourself," she often said. He believed her, and it frightened him. Syd even sometimes feared that she could read his mind. He had been faithful for thirty years of marriage—not because of any highly developed moral sense. He was a car salesman—how moral could he be? He was simply afraid of Ann.

Of course, there was that time in San Francisco. How long ago was it? Well, the boys were ten, so it was sixteen years ago—thirteen years into his marriage. Syd was alone, at a Honda party, when a striking Eurasian woman spoke to him. Two car sales pros making idle chitchat, he thought. It probably took him the longest time to catch on, he realized later, that something else was afoot. Too much eye contact. The personal space between them kept shrinking and shrinking. Soon, her hand was resting on his arm.

When it finally dawned on him that this woman *might* have an interest in him, he felt confused. There's a way to handle this, he thought to himself. He didn't want to make a fool of himself by inviting her to his room and getting rebuffed. It had been far too long since he'd been in this situation. Suddenly, he knew the answer. He knew just what he needed. He needed advice—but it had to be from someone smart, someone he could trust. Someone who understood him. He needed Ann. She's the one who has style, he thought. On the brink of what could have been a nicely frivolous one-night stand, Syd could only think of one thing: Ann would know the right thing to do. Not the right thing as in "Keep your pants zipped." But the right words, the proper way to invite her back to his room, what drinks to serve. Without Ann there to guide him, Syd felt too incompetent to have an affair. And calling her for advice just didn't seem practical.

So Syd behaved. He was tough at work and passive at home. He could yell at his employees but not his sons. He could say no in the midst of any negotiation and walk away without a grain of doubt. If Ann or the boys wanted something, however, he folded like a paper doll. It was his job to make them happy.

Syd had said nothing about the growing insurrection among the partners, but he knew Ann knew. "I bought you something," she'd said the other day, taking a break from her facial aerobics tape on TV. She presented him with a giant jar of Saint-John's-wort. It had helped, too.

Gladys buzzed in on the intercom. When Syd was behind closed doors, only seven callers were allowed to interrupt him—his four partners, his wife, and his two sons.

He was relieved to have it be Tim. "Dad, just a quick question. Do you have to be licensed to sell cars? I mean, if I wanted to sell cars out of my apartment, could I?"

"No, you'd need to have a license. You'd have to meet some fairly strict government guidelines, which would pretty much preclude you running things out of your apartment. They were designed as a way to keep Detroit from selling directly to the public, so there'd be an independent buffer between big powerful automakers and poor hapless consumers. That's why you have to have a place to show the cars, where people can drive them and see firsthand what they're buying. That's the law, at least in the state of California."

"Thanks, Dad. See you Sunday," said Tim, offering no insight on why he wanted the information in the first place. It was not Syd's nature to press, especially within the family. He was happy enough that Tim had called.

Besides, it took his mind off his problems. He packed up his briefcase, which, besides the notes from the meetings and some tax work, had the results of his newest nonhobby: gardening books, four of them.

# Passion Play

**For all the money** thrown around foolishly in Hollywood, surprisingly little of it is spent on interior design. Most offices are surprisingly Kmart-like, homogenous and functional and sometimes funky. The reason is simple. No one ever stays in an office long enough to do more than put up a poster of their last project and a picture of the family. If the job goes well, you get bumped up to a bigger, better office. If it doesn't, you move on to another characterless office at another studio. It drives the mail room guys crazy.

Jonathan Scott's office was befitting one of the 247 vice presidents who worked on the Sony lot. The title Vice President of Comedy Development for the Columbia TriStar Television Group was pretty much as low as you wanted to be in the studio system—senior vice president was, of course, better, and executive vice president better still. But to be a president was even cooler—after all, Sony, Columbia's parent company, had only twenty-six of those, one for each division, plus a few extras. The United States of America, by comparison, has one, but the world of fantasy is so much more complicated than the real world.

That Nancy and Perry's meeting was taking place in Jonathan's office was good—for Jonathan. It meant that executives from higher up in the food chain would be coming to his turf, a clear sign that *Dire Straights*, the pilot script, was his project.

As writers, Nancy and Perry were the first to arrive. A male assistant with a headset ushered them into Jonathan's office. The first thing Jonathan did, after pleasantries, was leave—having no intention of sitting in his own office with two writers. He skulked in the hall until his bosses arrived, running late as always.

"I think we can pretty much cut to the chase here," said Jonathan, leaning against his desk as Nancy and Perry sat on the couch and the two senior executives took the two chairs. "We've read what you've done and we feel passionate about it."

The others nodded in agreement as they scanned Perry's treatment.

"I believe it's important to go only with projects you feel passionate about," said Jonathan.

"Passion is what this business is all about," added one of the other executives. "Without passion, what do we have?"

"This whole concept is exactly what TV needs right now," said the other. "It's very fresh and yet traditional."

"That where the culture is right now," said Jonathan. "People want new things, but they want them to be familiar. That's why it's so easy to be passionate about this show."

"I consider myself a passion player," said Nancy firmly. "And I know this is the best work we've done. And there's no one I'd rather be in business with than Columbia. I wouldn't even take this project anywhere else."

Perry leaned forward to speak, but Nancy squeezed his knee in a none-too-subtle reminder that this was her turn. He was left to ponder how, exactly, he had managed to write something that was new and old at the same time.

Jonathan looked for a sign from the most senior executive. He received a slight nod.

"I think we're ready to put Comstock on the lot and tape this pilot. Our guys will do everything in their power to get this on a network for next season—and I think you both know that NBC owes us a big favor this year. I'd have no qualms calling in this favor on your show."

"That's fantastic," said Nancy. "We want partners who feel as strongly about this as we do."

Perry felt a bit of a squirm factor. He was all for schmoozing Hollywood types—he'd done his share of it—but Nancy was pouring it on bit heavy.

"We'll want protection, of course," she went on. "We have to be the show runners, or we'll take it elsewhere."

"That goes without saying," said Jonathan. "It's not just the script we're buying. It's you. It's your energy, your intensity, your . . ." He paused, not wanting to use the *P* word yet again, but the thesaurus in his mind faltered. "And yes, your passion. Heather says such great things about you, and you know how important her word is to us."

"I'm very glad to hear that," said Nancy. "We're not interested in a one-show arrangement. I have a notebook with dozens of good ideas, and after we prove ourselves to you with *Dire Straights*, we fully intend to gear up to do more shows and become a major force."

"That's the type of thinking we like to hear," said Jonathan.

She was clearly pleasing the two executives. In fact, everyone was happy but Perry, who wondered what these wonderful ideas were and who had come up with them. He hadn't, and Nancy certainly hadn't bothered burdening him with any ideas she might have had. Besides, wasn't he the creative force behind Comstock?

As congratulations were exchanged and arrangements made to bring the agents into this, Perry sat on the couch, stunned. *I sold a script,* he thought. *To a big studio.* His biggest credit so far had been the game show and writing smart-ass questions. Now he was a real writer. And very soon, he'd be a real producer.

"It was almost anticlimactic, wasn't it?" he said as they walked down the hall after the meeting. "I expected more. Maybe champagne. Confetti. Party favors."

"Didn't you feel the energy level in the room?" asked Nancy incredulously. "That was the most intense vibe I've ever felt. It was like the room was vibrating. Did you see how well I played them? I told them everything they wanted to hear. It was like I could read their minds."

"Maybe it hasn't sunk in yet," mused Perry. "What do we do now? Do you want to go to Starbucks or something?"

"We'll celebrate tonight. I've got to get back. And I should call Heather on the cell as soon as I get in the car. She's waiting to hear from me."

They kissed good-bye and Perry got in his Honda and drove off. When he got to the corner, he had an idea—perhaps they should do the Trader Vic's thing for dinner tonight, and invite some friends, maybe even his brother. He waited at the corner for Nancy's car. After a few minutes, when he saw no sign of her, he figured she had gone out another exit, and he moved on.

## Deep in the Vinyl Subculture

**It wasn't jealousy, exactly.** If it was, that wasn't a particularly good thing. Tim wanted to be happy for Perry's success, and on some level, he was. Perry was a good guy, a talented guy, a nice brother, and he deserved to have a show. But it all made Tim feel so terribly awful about his own life. Perry was on the brink of major money—if the show got on the air and lasted long enough to make it into syndication, Perry was looking at literally millions of dollars. Millions. Tim had just become comfortable with the idea that he lived in lower Los Angeles. That was okay, but he had figured Perry lived there, too. He assumed they'd both stay there—the idea of moving from lower to upper hadn't occurred to him. Nancy, on the other hand, was very upper L.A.—newly transplanted, totally smitten with Hollywood, with a brash and shallow attitude, like a bad imitation of a William Morris agent.

It didn't help that Tim was having this thought as he stacked all the free promotional CDs that he'd stored under his desk in a big box. Music companies loved to send out free CDs, even to entertainment Web sites, and in his short time at *Hollywood Today*, Tim had managed quite a collection, enough to warrant a trip to Record Surplus on Pico Boulevard.

Record Surplus was the rare record store that bought promotional CDs and paid cash for them. It was barely legal and certainly unethical for people to sell them, but everyone did it. Some record stores would take them only for credit. Tim, unlike his fabulously successful and better-looking brother, needed real money.

Record Surplus was famous for more than buying CDs. It was a paradise of vinyl, one of the last in the city. Rows and rows of actual record albums—big flat licorice pizzas—all of them used and sold to Record Surplus. Only a small corner of the store had the promotional CDs—it was a way of making sure that some current acts were available for the nondiscerning listener.

Tim deposited his box of CDs at the front desk, and while the clerk began a tally, Tim wandered around the store, looking at old Doors albums and reading liner notes. He glanced around at his fellow customers and felt like he had stumbled into a *Star Trek* convention. They were older guys, probably fortyish, with bad clothes, large stomachs, and neglected beards. Collectors, he thought. It didn't matter what guys collected—comic books, pinup photos, stamps, Zippo lighters—they all had that same look, as if they couldn't fit into the real world and so had found an acceptable subculture where they were welcome. Most of the customers browsed through the jazz albums—jazz fans being more inclined to insist on the purity of vinyl—but a couple of extremely large men were carefully examining comedy albums. Now there's a subsubculture—making sure you have a complete set of Allan Sherman or Stan Freberg on vinyl. This was clearly not a place for cruising, a sad fact, which both relieved and disappointed Tim. On one hand, he was feeling much better now that Sandy had done her makeover, a bit more stylish, a bit more desirable. Still, it was going to take more than new clothes to change his sorry social life.

Tim liked to push it from his mind, but it had now been a year since he'd been on a date or had a casual encounter. I have the sex drive of an eighty-year-old man, he thought, if that eighty-year-old was in a coma or suffering from advanced prostate cancer. Twice in the past year, he'd panicked and tried to fix the situation. First, he went to GNC in the Westside Pavilion and loaded up on yohimbine, probably the most highly touted and thus disappointing herbal aphrodisiac. It made him mildly hyper, but nothing more. During his second anxiety attack, he went to the Sepulveda West Car Wash, which not only gave the best state-of-the-art hot wax in town but was mysteriously filled with every New Age self-help book imaginable. In some ways, it was a better collection than the Bodhi Tree on Melrose. Probably the biggest difference between the two was that you left the Bodhi Tree in a cloud of incense and you left Sepulveda West with that great new-car smell.

It was fifteen dollars for the wash and fifty-two dollars' worth of books, all on his Unocal card. The books all pointed to his sagging self-esteem. Some books blamed his lack of spiritual fulfillment; others took a more psychological approach. It did give Tim a bit of a game plan. He'd have to become more successful. If he were more successful, he'd like himself more. Once that happened, everything would fall into place. But it was taking a painfully long time.

Back at the front counter at Record Surplus, Tim got the

bad news. There were two stacks of CDs. One was very short. The other was very tall.

"I can give you twelve dollars for these," said the clerk, pointing at the short stack.

"And those?" said Tim, hoping to be able to pay for a tank of gas at least.

"I don't want them," said the clerk. "You can take them. I've never heard of most of them."

Neither had Tim, but he had hoped he was simply unhip, rather than trying to unload worthless crap.

"You can keep them. They just take up room," said a defeated Tim, sighing.

"I'll tell you what," said the clerk. "We'll make it an even fifteen dollars."

"Thanks," said Tim, as he shoved the bills in his jeans pocket. This day had not been as profitable as he had hoped. It wouldn't even pay for half of one of the shirts Sandy had had him buy. It could never have been as profitable a day as Perry's.

## Perry's on Fire

**Even before the van** hit the impenetrable wall of traffic on Sunset Boulevard, everyone was in a snappish, surly mood. It wasn't just that it was day four of an unbearably hot, windy patch of weather. Barry was in a bad mood because he was the driver, the setting sun was hitting him square in the eyes, and he was driving his wife's minivan. He hated minivans. He hated that he owned one, but he'd been persuaded by the rest of the guys at *Boing!* to bring the van to work so they could all take one car to Perry's going-away bash at the beach. And if bringing the minivan wasn't bad enough, the fact that it was his car made him the de facto designated driver.

Lee, Jim, Tony, and Dick were pissed off, too. It was frustrating enough to watch one of their own—Perry, hardly the most talented of the group—leave the humble world of basic cable for a pilot at a real studio, but they also had to honor the guy, take him out for the traditional round of drinks at someplace outside the neighborhood, something that would be special, more of an occasion. Jim had innocently suggested Gladstone's 4 Fish, a tourist trap with mediocre food but strong tropical drinks and a great location on the beach, where Sunset Boulevard hits the Pacific Coast Highway. Since the beach is one of those mystical places that sounds great—until you actually face the bother of getting there—everyone immediately agreed. Shortly before they climbed in the van, they all silently realized what a huge mistake it was.

"Look, I found a pacifier," said Lee. "Can I use it? I can be like Snoop Dogg." The group marveled at it. Barry was slightly older—thirty-four—and came from the Midwest. Those two things were enough to make him a bit of an exotic, but his real oddity was his home life. In a profession that attracted perpetual adolescents eager to dedicate their every waking hour to career advancement, Barry went home around dinnertime. He had a wife, two children, and a house. Nothing could have been more alien than that.

"Leave the pacifier alone, please," said Barry, his voice betraying the stress of a man facing a night of watching his friends get drunk while he sipped diet Coke.

Perry kept checking his watch. He understood the tradition. It would have been an insult not to take him out for a farewell drink. He deserved that much, he figured. As the reality of his success sunk in, he was beginning to feel a bit proud. He even understood the jealousy and anger aimed his way from his former coworkers—that was probably the best part of the whole evening. The only thing he couldn't accept was the traffic gridlock.

"Turn on the radio," suggested Perry. "Let's see why we're not moving."

KFWB news radio promised that if you gave them twenty-two minutes, they'd give you the world. Mostly, though, they gave you traffic and weather. Being Los Angeles, traffic was far more important than real news anyway, so KFWB thoughtfully updated their traffic reports at seven-minute intervals, leaving only a small amount of time for world and national events. That suited everyone just fine.

It didn't take twenty-two minutes to get the world. It didn't even take seven. Barry pushed the first button on the mini-van's radio and got an instantaneous update. "And, of course, that raging brush fire in Malibu is making a mess out of traffic on the Pacific Coast Highway," announced KFWB's news reader. "The Highway Patrol has closed off traffic at Topanga, so be prepared for serious delays if you're headed in that direction."

Usually, fires in Malibu are no inconvenience to the general population. In fact, on the long list of multiple natural disasters that strike Southern California regularly, they are among the most entertaining. They make for great TV, they always include an impressive celebrity quotient (what could be better than watching a panicked David Hasselhoff hosing down his mansion with a green garden hose—the only time he had touched any piece of his own yard equipment since moving to Malibu?), and, better yet, brush fires are a nicely localized problem. If you live in West L.A., the fire might as well be in the Pacific Northwest. The only way you know L.A. is in the throes of peril is that regular TV programming is pre-empted and replaced with team coverage of brave firefighters and spunky celebrities fighting to save their multimillion-dollar estates. Fires make for much better TV than earthquakes, since earthquakes strike with no warning and are over before the average TV commercial. Fires rage on for days, they involve dramatic water-dropping aircraft, and they're somewhat pretty, if you can forget the downside.

"Should we turn around?" asked Barry, being the practical one.

Lee, Jim, Tony, and Dick were feeling more adventurous. The idea of sitting at a bar, pounding back vodka martinis, listening to the sirens as neighboring fire departments raced to help, watching team coverage on the TV over the bar—it all sounded good to them. Perry voted to proceed, as well. He didn't want to be cheated out of his moment just because a few beach houses were burning to the ground and the traffic was thick with fire trucks.

Johnny Carson, Dick Clark, Barbra Streisand, David Geffen, Martin Sheen—the news anchors sounded like they were hawking maps to the stars' homes. Those were the homes in danger, they said. Not "immediate danger," as it turned out. The fire was currently burning in a remote area of Decker Canyon, a bit north of Malibu's celebrity enclave and more where the other half of the population live. Like so many areas of Los Angeles, Malibu contains two distinct and separate communities—a wealthy, high-profile contingent and, surprisingly, a rural, almost redneck segment, many of whom have lived in Malibu with their horses and livestock in ramshackle housing for generations. They all coexist nicely, shopping at the same markets, sending their kids to the same public schools (Malibu has probably the best public schools in the area), and joining hands to fight fires, sandbag against floods, and argue against overdevelopment.

Even though the fire was in its infancy—threatening homes, not burning them to the ground—the team coverage had an odd effect on Perry and his friends. It made them jealous.

"I'd love to move Eloise and the kids out to Malibu." Barry sighed. "The schools are so good and the air is so clean."

"Don't property values drop after a fire like this?" asked

Lee. "Couldn't we all afford a nice beachfront condo? Aren't all these rich idiots fleeing for Beverly Hills right now?"

"People in Malibu never move," said Tony. "The house burns down and they rebuild it. A big wave demolishes their front deck and they replace it with a bigger deck. The rains fill their living rooms with mud and they just buy new Oriental rugs. They're insanely loyal."

"And insanely rich," added Jim.

Perry didn't say anything, but it occurred to him that Malibu was at best a pipe dream for everyone else from *Boing!* Now that he was a show runner, he was the only one actually in a position to afford the Malibu lifestyle, and, fires or no, the idea suddenly had a certain appeal.

# The Great Delicatessen Wars Claim Another Casualty

**There was disagreement in** the air when Ann attended her first meeting of CUSS, Citizens United for the Study of Secession, but it had little to do with politics. Instead, the heated discussion around the sunken Sherman Oaks living room, with its gigantic sectional sofa, oversized ficus tree, and big-screen TV, centered on food. Linda, the chapter chairperson and hostess, had brought in a tray from Jerry's Delicatessen in Studio City. However, a vocal minority felt strongly that Art's Delicatessen, a mile or so farther east, would have been a smarter, tastier choice.

"There's no getting around it," said one woman. "Jerry's is a *chain.*" She uttered that last word disdainfully, as if "chain" food was prechewed and filled with rat hair.

"There's only one Art's," pointed out another woman. "It's a family operation. It shows."

"Where every sandwich is a work of Art," added another woman, feeling the necessity to throw in Art's shopworn motto for lack of anything original to say.

Ann was firmly with the Art's rebels, but she remained quiet, conserving her energy for the rigorous political debate she knew would follow. She found it odd that the group was so small, and that it was all women—all upper-middle-class white women driving SUVs and wearing gold earrings. Not that women can't move mountains, mind you, but she expected that something so highly charged and political would be, well, more coed. Maybe even a tad more diverse. But that wasn't important. Ann had questions, about schools, taxes, police, the fire department—splitting the Valley off from the rest of Los Angeles seemed fraught with peril. What form of government would the new city have? Is it like a divorce? Will the powers that run Los Angeles try to pawn off the old, ineffective street-cleaning machines on the new city, keeping the good stuff for itself? Will secession happen overnight? Will the Valley go to bed on a Tuesday night and wake up Wednesday morning with a new mayor, new city council, new fire and police chief, and new superintendent of schools? Or do cities secede gradually, one department at a time? What about the Dodgers and LACMA? Can you have a custody fight over a baseball team and an art museum? Why is all the good stuff on *that* side of the hill, anyway? Maybe USC or UCLA could move to the Valley. Certainly USC would be interested—it's in such a terrible part of town.

Those were the questions haunting Ann. The questions haunting the rest of the group had more to do with latkes. The superiority of Art's latkes versus the pathetic attempts at Jerry's.

"What do you expect from Jerry's?" asked one woman. "It's inside a bowling alley." The group nodded, sadly acknowledging the bitter truth of that statement. Jerry's did indeed share a building with a bowling alley.

Ann felt that perhaps she should speak up. "How soon before the meeting actually begins?" she asked, carefully using a therapeutic tone of voice so that her question would sound nonthreatening.

The group grew silent as they pondered how to tell the new person that this *was* the meeting.

Finally, one of the women spoke. "One of things we try to do here is build a sense of community. We've been the bastard stepchild of Los Angeles for so long, we forget that we have an identity."

"And power," added another.

"Our agenda is not a downtown businessman's agenda. We're not obsessed with power. We want to build something, not tear down."

To Ann, this was beginning to sound like those feminist meetings she had gone to at Everywoman's Village when the boys were young. That's not such a bad thing, she thought. She had appreciated the sense of community she had gotten there, and if CUSS gave her the same thing, she'd be ahead of the game. She still loved Everywoman's Village, after all. The pottery class she took there was better than therapy. Besides, everyone loved the series of decorative bowls she made in that class and her teacher wondered why she didn't try to sell them.

One woman began to tear up. "Perhaps you're new to the Valley," she said to Ann. "Perhaps you haven't had to live with the low self-esteem and self-loathing the way the rest of us have."

Before Ann could protest, the woman held up her hand.

"I'm going to make a confession now. I'm going to tell this room something I never, ever talk about." The group again became quiet as it prepared to share. "Years ago, after my second baby was born, my husband and I prepared a will. We wanted to make sure that if, God forbid, something bad happened to us, our children would be well cared for." The audience murmured its approval.

"But we had a decision to make. Who would take care of the kids if we died? Would it be my parents—two wonderful people who loved and cared for our children deeply, who lived right here in Sherman Oaks and saw the children often? Or would it be his parents—cold, wealthy, self-absorbed Gentiles who lived in Holmby Hills?"

Even Ann found herself leaning forward to hear more.

"When we filed that will, I did something I will be forever ashamed of. I agreed with my husband that his parents should get guardianship of our children—not because they were better people, not because they were rich—but because . . ."

She pointed a finger in Ann's direction.

"But because I didn't want my children to grow up in the Valley if they didn't have to!"

Several small gasps filled the room, followed by sotto voce expressions of support and understanding.

"To me, that's why we're here. So that no mother will ever be forced to make the choice I had to make."

Even Ann realized that all the air had been sucked out of the room and that any sensible discussion was now impossible, so she got up and made herself a sandwich from the Jerry's deli platter.

There is no getting around it, she thought. Art's is definitely the better deli.

## The Lord of the Gym Knows All

**It wasn't just the** awkwardness he felt from Tim but also the awkwardness—resentment, even—Perry felt from the world at large that was so bothersome. Tim's reaction was easy to understand—what brothers aren't plagued by sibling rivalry? It wasn't as if things were going great for Tim. The guys at work, the other writers who were busy trying to sell their screenplays . . . well, of course they'd have mixed emotions. Suddenly, everyone was behaving differently, and Perry had barely moved into his new office. His parents acted as if he was already rich, old friends hinted around for jobs while making sarcastic asides about his dumb luck, newer friends pretended they'd been friends for years, and, in the most surreal moment, his agent called—*just to say hi.*

It didn't matter much what time you showed up at 24-Hour Fitness: Peter—the lord of the gym—was there, wandering from machine to machine, playing racquetball, drinking a Snapple at the snack bar. Mostly, though, Peter chatted. Stout, muscular, and in his early fifties, he introduced himself as a TV producer. While he used the present tense and he did maintain a small office at one of the studios, his career seemed to exist well in the past, during the golden age of variety shows, back when Dinah Shore was a singer, not a dead lesbian icon. When Regis Philbin was lucky to be a sidekick. Back before Donny and Marie had emotional problems they happily shared on *Entertainment Tonight*. Back before Cher had tattoos and Sonny took ski lessons. Peter hadn't had a show on the air since the eighties, but he'd apparently made good money while he could—he drove an elegant Mercedes and had plenty of free time. In any given three-hour span, he might work out for twenty minutes. However, he knew everyone and picked up on every speck of gossip.

"I can't figure out why Nancy would hire the likes of you to work on her show," said Peter.

"She has no choice," said Perry. "I'm the brains of the operation. I wrote the script."

"Yes, and we all know how powerful a writer is in Hollywood," said Peter.

Perry laughed. "It's just a commitment to do a pilot. There are no guarantees," he said, mentally knocking on wood.

"That's a good way of looking at it," said Peter. "It's a great first step—not that many people get to do pilots. There are a lot people involved in pilots who find themselves back waiting tables when the pilot doesn't sell."

"Or writing game-show questions." Perry nodded.

"What's your role now that the script is written?"

"Nancy and I will be the show runners. We'll start casting

in the next couple of weeks and shoot the pilot as is. If it goes, it goes—and then I'll have a TV show, I guess."

"Be careful," warned Peter. "Lots of things can go wrong. You're going to be dealing with a lot of people who will be looking out for themselves. You have to watch out for yourself, okay?"

And Nancy, thought Perry. I have to watch out for the two of us. Especially now, since Nancy had been behaving so oddly. Instead of bringing them closer, success seemed to be a big distraction. They'd had dinner only once since the fateful meeting—Nancy was constantly busy—and their phone conversations were hurried and unsatisfying. When he'd try to talk, she'd sound annoyed and impatient, always eager to get back to Heather. She was rushed when they talked business and she had no time whatsoever for any of that mushy stuff that's part of a normal relationship. Perry sometimes feared that while he was looking for a girlfriend, Nancy wanted to be more of a business partner. The sad thing was that Perry often doubted whether she was all that suited for either role.

When he got back to his apartment, there were eight messages waiting for him. One was from Tim, who said he had convinced Simon James to do a small feature on Perry's new show for *Hollywood Today*. There was a forced cheerfulness in Tim's voice, but Perry was impressed that, as envious as he was, Tim was still capable of a brotherly gesture.

Of course, there were two calls from Nancy—her voice racing, her tone urgent. "Heather has some more really good casting ideas. I really want you to hear them," she said in her first message. "I can't make dinner tonight—sorry, hon," said the second message. "Heather needs me to go with her to the Garden of Eden tonight. She has to see her ex and it's freaking her out."

Mom had called, announcing a special Sunday dinner

("Your dad is taking us all out to Casa Vega," she said excitedly), and Dad had called in his typically car-centered way ("It occurred to me that you might be thinking of getting rid of the Civic, and I wanted to remind you that I can get you a good deal on an Accord, or, if you wanted, an Acura").

The remaining three calls came from friends, who had heard it through the grapevine. It was male bonding at its best—not one of them could actually muster congratulations without sarcasm. Paul, his basketball buddy, had it down.

"Whoa, they've lowered the bar. A comedy? You're only funny when you play basketball, and you get your biggest laughs when you get hurt. You, sir, are the Steve Guttenberg of writers—a no-talent who succeeds where we hardworking artistic types fail. So congratulations, and don't forget all those times you promised me a job. As luck would have it, I'm available."

# Bagels and Art

**Sandy's head popped over** the cubicle wall. "How much do you love bad art?"

"I adore bad art," said Tim. "What's not to love about bad art?"

"A friend of mine who's a wonderfully bad artist—and also something of a bad friend—is having a bad art opening tonight and I really have to go; otherwise, I'd be as bad a friend as she is. And if you went with me, it wouldn't be quite so bad."

"How badly do you want me to go?" asked Tim dryly.

"So badly that I'll buy you dinner," Sandy said earnestly. "I'll take you to Kate Mantilini's and buy you a really good burger."

"As I'm sure you know, I'm extremely sought after as a

friend, lover, and companion. What makes you assume I'm free tonight?"

"I already checked your calendar and saw a big blank space," said Sandy. "I didn't feel like facing rejection."

"So no excuse I could muster would be believable at this point?"

"None. You're sorta stuck."

"In that case," said Tim magnanimously, "I'd love to go. What gallery?"

"It's not a gallery," said Sandy. "We're talking bad art. We're going to Bagelteria."

"Perfect," said Tim. "I've never been to an actual art gallery, so my streak remains intact. And I love bagels."

It was true. Tim had now been to several art openings, and not one of them had been in an actual gallery. Sandy, who had far too many artists as friends, found herself in galleries only a sliver of the time she spent looking at her friends' work. She'd been to art openings at hair salons, snack bars, a dry cleaner's, a vitamin store–cum–homeopathic pharmacy, a patio furniture outlet, and dozens of restaurants. As art became just another form of mass entertainment for the postcollege crowd, it seemed as if you could find—and buy—art anywhere. The local museums, like the Los Angeles County Museum of Art and downtown's Museum of Contemporary Art, caught on to this new trend in a nanosecond, offering free outdoor concerts and doing everything they could to lure a younger crowd. That made LACMA one of the premier date-night activities in L.A.—it presented just the right image, especially since that whole Friday-evening crowd looked like they came straight from the Standard on its way to the SkyBar.

The old-line galleries, however, missed the trend entirely. They lacked those savvy, high-powered marketing staffs that the museums needed to stay alive. They couldn't figure out a way to make it a party, leaving a void in the marketplace that was quickly filled by a couple of bright entrepreneurs. For 15 percent (less than a gallery takes), they matched up a business with empty wall space with a struggling artist. The businesses, especially restaurants, got an ever-changing art show (plus 10 percent of any sales); the artists had numerous opportunities to show their work all over town. It was surprising how many people would shell out $650 impulsively for the painting that hung over their plate of tagliatelle and scallops. It was all such fun that parties sprang up whenever new art arrived, and everybody liked that fine, too.

"So why are we doing this again?" asked Tim, taking a bite of his Kate Mantilini burger.

"Jean is a friend from art school, and I'm showing support, even though I want her to fail."

"I didn't know you went to art school," said Tim. "Are you an artist?"

"Look at yourself," said Sandy indignantly. "You look wonderful. Why? Because of my artistic eye. Now tell me, have you gotten compliments?"

"I'm fighting off potential suitors with a tire iron," he said. "But I'm not your only canvas. Or am I?"

"I retired young. I wanted to waste four years of art school as part of my campaign to drive my parents crazy."

"Is it working?"

"My father is immune to all outside forces and my mother is already crazy, so it's something of an empty gesture on my part."

"Clearly, you're an only child. Driving parents crazy is best as a tag-team sport. It's too exhausting otherwise. When all else fails, that's what brings Perry and me together—the united front against the parental unit."

Sandy was picking at her Life Rice, Kate Mantilini's low-fat, low-cal, low-taste, low-guilt specialty.

"Why did you really quit?" asked Tim.

"Quit what?" replied Sandy, genuinely baffled.

"Art. It couldn't have been money—no matter how little you made as an artist, it has to match what Simon pays us. You must have quit for a reason."

"I don't know," Sandy said with a shrug. "I think it became too important. When I painted, I drove myself crazy. Not painting drove my folks crazy. It was an easy choice."

"Do you miss it?"

"I will tonight, when I see everyone. I'll feel like a failure for a while, but it'll pass."

"That's where you're lucky being an only child. I get to feel like a failure *and* watch my brother become the new David E. Kelley," said Tim. "Trust me, that's pain."

"Have you noticed that David Kelley has a quickly growing bald spot?" asked Sandy. "You could see it on the Emmys. It's quite at odds with that tousled mop head thing he has going."

"Really." Tim was genuinely intrigued. "I'll have to tell Perry. He has a David Kelley fixation and a hair fixation—this is the best of two worlds for him."

"Why does your brother have a hair fixation? He has great hair. You both do."

"He's always been in a panic about losing his hair. He spends a fortune feeding it Miracle-Gro for hair. You know how some guys are about their prize lawns. That's Perry and his hair. He'd enter it in the county fair if he could."

"Does it really make you jealous that he sold a show?"

Tim paused to measure his words precisely. "Just once, I'd like us both to be successful. I just want one family dinner when it's equal. I don't want to feel sorry for myself, and I don't even like feeling sorry for him. But I really hate Mom and Dad feeling sorry for me."

"Poor Tim, the failure boy?"

"My mother told me I was a late bloomer," said Tim, shaking his head. "That's her way of encouraging me."

"You're lucky," said Sandy. "The only thing my mom ever encouraged me to do was lose weight."

"But you look great. You don't have a weight problem at all. You have a fantastic figure—and I'm not even trying to seduce you."

Sandy laughed. "Maybe I try to please my parents more than I think."

## Syd Goes on a Date

**For Syd, it was** almost like a date. He took extra care choosing his wardrobe—he wanted to wear nothing that made the wrong statement. He trimmed his nose hair, even though it wasn't a weekend, and put drops in his eyes so he'd look alert, not tired. He thought long and hard before making reservations for lunch at Tony Roma's. He so bubbled with enthusiasm, it was hard for Gladys to ignore.

"You're just like a little kid," she said. "It's so adorable."

"What's with him?" asked the sales manager.

"Syd has a special lunch today," said Gladys. "He's excited."

Syd blushed, smiled awkwardly, and retreated into the sanctity of his plush office. He hid there, watching the clock, checking the stock market on his computer, pricing airfares to Hawaii and pondering his nonexistent garden. It seemed as if 12:30 would never come.

Finally, he heard Gladys shriek with delight. There was laughter, and a small congregation of some of the longtime employees came around to say hi, slap backs, make jokes. Syd relaxed—any fear of a last minute cancellation had vanished. He stayed quietly in his office. It would cause the group to scatter if he came out, and he wanted his guest to have a few moments to catch up.

"Okay, everybody, back to work," said Gladys, clapping her hands. "Your dad has been so excited about your lunch. I swear, I've never seen a father more attached to his two boys."

"What's not to love?" joked Perry. "Well, Tim's sort of moody, but I'm the best lunch in town."

He knocked and opened the door simultaneously.

"Hi, Dad," he said. They hugged and Perry scanned the room. "It's like a sky box at Staples Center. All you need is a wet bar."

It has been a long time since either of the boys had come to the dealership. When they were still living at home, they were both underfoot constantly, growing up in the showroom, bringing out the rarely seen human side of the car salesmen who came and went. They spent summers working in the service center and were the most voracious customers the vending machines would ever see. But now, Tim and Perry showed up only when it was time to trade in one Honda Civic for another, and recently, they just both assumed when it was time for a new car—the one perk the family enjoyed—that Syd would bring it home and they'd swap during Sunday dinner. This time, though, Perry had simply called and invited himself to lunch without any ulterior motive—at least as far as Syd knew.

There was so much Syd wanted to show Perry, but he didn't want to seem overeager. "Do you want to see the new security cameras?" asked Syd anxiously.

Perry's face lit up. He had a bit of a techno fetish, and Dad had described the new system with such enthusiasm over dinner once that Perry had actually dreamed about it that night.

"Look there," said Syd as they left the office, pointing to what looked like a smoke detector in the ceiling above Gladys.

Perry looked. "A camera?" he guessed. Indeed. There were cameras all over the place, feeding to a bank of monitors and VCRs in a room in the back. There wasn't much need for them during the day, but at after closing, the night watchman could keep his eye on every corner of the lot without leaving his chair. What had thrilled Perry, though, and fed his dreams was the fact that the cameras—unbeknownst to anyone—also fed into the TV in the inner sanctum. When he so desired, Syd could click through channels that showed him his entire empire and everyone in it. At first, he was hooked on it—spying constantly from his big leather chair. But like Internet porn or Fox TV shows, it got old fast. He was more likely to watch Judge Judy than Newman Super Honda any day.

"I'm taking the red S2000 to lunch," Syd said to Gladys as he left.

"I thought you would." She smiled.

As befitting a family with a car dealership, none of the Newmans were serious car people. They viewed cars practically—as transportation and not much more. Still, the S2000 was a kick for anyone to drive, and Syd wanted Perry to have fun.

"I guess you'll be able to afford one of these soon," Syd mentioned in passing.

"It's crossed my mind," said Perry. "If this show goes, a lot might change. I'll probably move—maybe even buy something, even if it's just a condo in Malibu—and I'm definitely going to join a better gym. Maybe Sports Club/L.A.—it's a fortune, but I hear it's well worth it."

At lunch, the real reason for Perry's appearance started to emerge. Both boys were constant mysteries to Syd, no matter how much energy he invested in figuring them out. This time, Perry's concerns were painfully clear.

"Do you know when Mom gets in those moods, those moods where she just doesn't want to talk and gets totally obsessed by her job of the moment? Do you ever worry that she's not in love with selling real estate or being a therapist, but just hates you instead?" Perry asked, well into the meal and after much diversionary chatter.

"Hates me?" said Syd, a bit surprised. Ann was a bit compulsive, but he never interpreted it as hate. "Your mom is just single-minded sometimes. Lots of people are."

Perry was flustered. "But how would you know? How can you be sure which is the overriding emotion? Does she love a certain project? Or is she really escaping you?"

Syd suppressed a laugh. "At a certain point in their lives, all the women I know have a need to escape. A lot of the men I know do, too. They're looking for something better in life. Sometimes that something better is really some*one* better. But usually, it's not. It's a job, or a hobby or a project or a trip. Once your family is grown, you have lots of time to kill—especially if you're not working."

"Does it scare you when Mom is unhappy?"

"A little. But when she's like that, it's not that she's unhappy with me. It's other aspects of her life. At least that's what I tell myself," explained Syd. "And it's not unhappiness. It's dissatisfaction. After all, it's not like your mother has ever found herself."

"But don't you feel like that's your fault?"

"No, but I think she does," said Syd, and they both laughed.

"Does she ever not talk to you for long periods of time?"

"No, that's one thing I can say. Even when she's in the worst mood in the world, we always talk. We've never not talked."

"What do you talk about?"

"Not her problems, necessarily. She has her special interests—age, weight. We talk about you boys a lot."

"How come you're satisfied with life and Mom isn't?"

"Men just embrace dullness better. It's in our genes. Your mother sees life like a game of draw poker. She always wants a way to improve her hand. Remember when we used to travel and the first hotel room was never good enough for her? That's also why we change tables in restaurants. My life is more like five-card stud. I play the cards I'm dealt."

The minute Perry was gone and Syd was back in his office, he called Ann. There was an unspoken agreement that any information involving the boys had to be downloaded immediately. "I just had lunch with Perry. I think there are problems between him and Nancy."

"He told you that?" Ann was incredulous.

"In his own roundabout way, yes," said Syd. "I gathered they're serious problems."

By the time she hung up, Ann was so stressed, she was glad she had started taking SAM-e to even out her mood swings. Just when things were going so well for Perry, too.

She was also a little jealous of Syd. Perry would never be so open with her, and she was the one with therapeutic training.

## Greetings from Lower Los Angeles

**"How is life in** upper Los Angeles?" asked Tim.

Perry could answer that question in so many ways: He could say, It sucks, which, given the odd turn his relationship with Nancy was taking, would be true. He could say, It's great, which was also accurate enough. In a world in which all waiters, secretaries, and car mechanics are poised over their i-Macs, churning out enough screenplays to decimate the rain forest, Perry had done something neat—he had sold a half-hour sitcom to a big-time studio, and no matter what happened, even if the show was never picked up by a network, he'd see his pilot episode produced, his lines spoken by real actors on a real set, and he'd have an office on the Sony lot, with business cards that read "Executive Producer."

"It reads better than it lives," he told Tim, taking the writerly way out.

"Shouldn't you be deliriously happy?" asked Tim. "Shouldn't you and Nancy be hanging out at Morton's with David Kelley and Michelle Pfeiffer?"

"I probably should be deliriously happy, but I'm not. Things are weird with Nancy—I mean, I can't tell you how weird. Wait—I can. Here's how weird they are. I went and had lunch with Dad and asked him about women. That's how weird they are."

"Dad? Our dad?"

"Yes, Syd Newman, owner of the Valley's third-largest Honda dealership and husband of the bossiest woman in all of Studio City."

"What advice could Dad possibly give? Roll over and play dead—it's worked for me?"

"He didn't say much, but that was the gist," said Perry. "You know Syd—in his eyes, Ann can do no wrong."

"You could have come to me. I'm your age at least. I'm hurt."

"You're gay."

"We have feelings. You could argue we have more feelings, especially me. I have way too many feelings. Anyway, just because I'm gay shouldn't disqualify me. At least disqualify me for a good reason—like my total failure at any relationships whatsoever."

"Well, there is that."

"I still want to help. Not that I want to be competitive with Dad, of all people—although that might be less intimidating than competing with you. But I know lots of stuff. I watch a lot of TV. I have all his relationship information, from Lucy and Ricky to Will and Grace. It's all stored upstairs and available for you, as my brother."

"I write TV, remember?"

"Oh, yes, that does cheapen it, doesn't it? Just think, my entire worldview has been formed by people like you. No wonder I'm fucked up."

"You're a paragon of normalcy compared to my girlfriend-slash-partner."

"So how bad is it? And what happens with the show if you two aren't getting along?"

"I haven't seen her and she's too busy to talk. A wall has gone up, and I don't know why. I don't know how bad it is and I don't know what will happen. Maybe I'm making it out to be more than it is. I just don't know," said Perry.

"I would guess success would throw people for a loop, at least initially," offered Tim. "Not that I have any firsthand experience, but it seems to me they've done TV movies on that.

"Listen," continued Tim. "Why don't you just go and talk to her? Drive over there, to Heather's house or wherever she is, and just sit down and talk. What's the worst that can happen?"

While a dramatic entrance into Heather's guest house was not exactly Perry's style, Tim's advice made a certain amount of sense. Not the type of sense that would hold up to careful scrutiny, Perry knew, so if he was going to follow it, he'd better do so now, before he talked himself out of it. He drove to Laurel Canyon, took a left on Kirkwood, and went to the strange cul-de-sac. There, perched on the impossibly steep hill, were four houses, each reachable by its own funicular. The house on the far right belonged to Heather. Perry got in the funicular and pressed the buzzer. Usually, a voice—often Nancy's—would come on the intercom and ask, "Who is it?" This time, the funicular simply started its ascent.

Perry went around the back to the guest house and knocked on the door. "Oh, hi Perry," said Heather. "Nancy's not here. She's off at the studio. I don't expect her back until four or so. I'll tell her you were here."

"Oh, great—thanks," stammered Perry. "I'll see you later."

"I guess you will, now that we're going to be working together and all."

Perry felt himself go into blink mode—an involuntary spasm of eye twitches when he was forced to process too much information at once.

"Working together?"

"Yes, I know everyone's surprised that I'd even think about doing a sitcom at this point in my life, but something really feels right about it."

"My sitcom? *Dire Straights*?"

"I think it will be fun. Fun is a good thing. And I haven't had much fun lately."

On the ride down the funicular, Perry thought briefly of jumping overboard. It wouldn't work well as a suicide attempt—he'd just roll down the hill and mess up his clothes—but it seemed so appropriate.

What is Heather doing in *my* TV show? he wondered angrily. There's not one role that's even remotely appropriate for her. Not one. And why didn't Nancy tell me about this?

His mind raced, computing all the possibilities. Had Nancy sold him out, and made some sort of side deal with Heather? Did Columbia and Jonathan Scott know about this? Or was Nancy humoring Heather? That was entirely possible—Nancy had built a career on placating Heather, making her believe she was getting her way, only to manipulate her deftly in an entirely different direction. But if that was the case, why hadn't Nancy told him? It would have been good for a laugh, if nothing else.

What was it that Tim had said? "Just sit down and talk. What's the worst that can happen?" Sometimes, Tim can be such an idiot, thought Perry.

## The Secret Box in Tim's Closet

**Tim was the first** to admit that of all the childish, embarrassing, teenage, imbecilic fixations one can have in life, he had the worst. A crush so stupid and so humiliating, he told no one. Even in his small single apartment, where few outsiders ever ventured, he kept the evidence under a layer of old sweaters, in a taped box in the back corner of his closet, actually closing the curtains before he'd take the box out and undo the tape. And always, when he was done, he'd replace the pictures just as they'd been, on the bottom of the box, sweaters on top, lid securely taped shut.

How and why Tim had developed his crush on Kato Kaelin was a mystery, even to Tim. At first, during the O. J. trial, Kato was just another character, one Tim hardly noticed. When the media turned Kato into a major player, Tim became slowly fascinated and then sadly and inexplicably hooked. Forget the entire cast of *Dawson's Creek;* Kato was Tim's fantasy guy—cute, fun, with a great body. Stupid, too—Tim knew that, but it didn't bother him. Over the years, he had collected articles about Kato, mainly for the pictures. The shirtless ones were his favorites, and he had a surprising number of them, proving to Tim that he was not alone in his fixation. Magazine editors had the same problem. Once, Kato spent a half hour shirtless on *Politically Incorrect*—they said it was some sort of beach-theme show, but Tim assumed he had yet another kindred spirit out there, one who was able turn his fascination into televised reality. Tim kept a tape of that show in the box, too.

Perry was vaguely aware of Tim's crush. Once, when Tim went on an involuntary Kato-related talking jag, Perry looked at him and said, "Well, he has great hair—I'll give him that."

That's why it was so odd to have Sandy suspend a copy of *Maxim,* open to a photo spread of Kato, the same feature Tim had cut out and put in his box just the night before, over the cubicle wall and ask, "Doesn't he just give you the creeps?"

"I don't fully understand everyone's fascination with him," said Tim insincerely. "He's just accidentally famous. I don't know why he hasn't faded away. You see his name every-where."

"He's such a loser," she said emphatically. "But he is sorta cute." She sat back down.

Tim's intercom buzzed, and Simon, his voice raspy and punctuated with coughs, asked him to come to his office im-mediately.

"I'm supposed to be a guest on a radio show today, and I thought I'd be up to it. But as this morning goes on, my cold feels worse and worse. I hate to put you in this position, but I need you to fill in for me. It's Warren Olney's show, *Which Way LA?* You've heard of it, I'm sure. He's doing a show about the Internet. Matt Drudge will be there and some woman with a sex site. And you, of course. Have you ever been on radio?"

Tim shook his head.

"It's surprisingly painless, and you're the right person. It'll be good for us, and frankly, it'll be good for you. There's one slight drawback. . . ."

"Yes?"

"You'll need to be at KCRW in an hour—and that's in Santa Monica, so you might want to leave immediately. I'm sorry I didn't give you more notice. These colds can really sneak up on you."

"Wow, a radio show. This is as close to upper L.A. as I'll ever get."

Simon smiled. "It's as close as you'll want to be."

The next fifteen minutes were a flurry of activity, with Sandy agreeing to tape the show ("Why are you teacher's pet?" she asked. "Why not me?" "Because you thought Marilyn Manson was a girl," answered Tim), a quick phone call to his mom, who volunteered to call the others, and then the drive to the radio station, his mind racing.

Once he was there, it was all surprisingly low-key and casual. No one rushed, even with airtime seconds away. People walked in and out of the studio, bringing coffee and water, while the show was on the air live.

It all happened too quickly for Tim to get nervous. Well, not overly nervous at any rate. And he learned a lot. He learned that even when you're on an hour-long radio show, you don't get to talk much. A few sentences go a long way. He got to see Matt Drudge wrestle with the dilemma of how to fit the headphones over his trademark fedora. Ultimately, he gave up and took off the hat. He saw how polished and poised Danni of Danni's Hard Drive was—for a porn star, she was the smoothest talker of the group, except for Olney. Most of all, he learned that he could do it: He could go on a radio talk show and not embarrass himself.

When he returned to the office and got a round of applause from the staff and saw the phone messages from his mother, father, brother, and several friends, he realized something else: A little bit of fame is a great thing.

## Girls Just Want to Have Fun

**Perry called his agent.** He was unavailable. He called Jonathan Scott. Unavailable. He called Nancy several times. Extremely unavailable. Finally, at 11:00 P.M., feeling too low to talk and too wired to sleep, he turned off the ringer on his phone and took two Dalmane—a potent dose for anyone—and sought refuge in sleep.

He awoke to the sound of his fax machine. Tim was faxing the front page of *The Hollywood Reporter*:

## THE *Hollywood* REPORTER

### Heather Windward in Dire Straights

Gen-X poster girl Heather Windward has taken an interesting career switch by agreeing to exec-produce and star in a sitcom, *Dire Straights*, for Columbia TriStar's TV unit, with a guaranteed berth on NBC in the fall. The show's cocreator and co—executive producer is longtime Windward associate Nancy Marshall, under the Kirkwood Productions banner, a company the duo formed last month.

"I think it's time in my life to have to some fun," said Windward. "And I think this show will be different enough to provide the creative challenge it's so hard to get in movies today."

Based loosely on an original script by Marshall and game-show scribe Perry Newman, the show is undergoing a complete revise, with veteran TV hand Babaloo Mandel working with Marshall on a new, hipper version.

"With Heather on board, we have a chance to push the sitcom envelope," said Jonathan Scott, VP of Comedy Development at Columbia TriStar. "The original pilot was in some ways too traditional. We all want to see something very young and cutting-edge."

There was no point in calling Nancy. His rage at her was so intense, there was nothing she could do or say that wouldn't make him even angrier. There are broken hearts, and there's being used and made to be the fool. It wasn't until this moment that Perry realized how much worse the latter could be.

Perry called his agent first. "I haven't been looking forward to this conversation," said the agent. "This is just one of those ugly things that happens. It happens to everyone sometime or other. Just be thankful you hadn't devoted your life to this before the ax fell. Besides, if the show goes, you'll have some back-end participation. It'll be found money. Mailbox money. The best kind."

Jonathan Scott was next. "I have to tell you, I've been dreading this phone call," said Jonathan. "This has been a very awkward situation for all of us. We all loved your script, but once Nancy brought us Heather and we saw the synergistic possibilities of that relationship, we had to make some changes."

"But why were those changes made without me? I was the goddamn show runner! I wrote the goddamn script!"

Jonathan took a deep breath. "I was led to believe that Nancy was the real creative force behind the concept," he said.

"Frankly, Perry, you were so quiet in the meeting that we assumed you lacked real passion for the project. Nancy, on the other hand, was virtually on fire. That's what it takes to get things done."

"But why wasn't I told?" Perry demanded. "I had a right to be kept in the loop."

"Nancy said she was taking care of it," said Jonathan. "I had no reason to doubt her."

"She didn't take care of it. I read it in *The Hollywood Reporter* this morning."

"That must have hurt," consoled Jonathan. "But listen, you have friends here. We'd love to be in business with you. You'll have other ideas, and we'll talk. I know this must be painful, but it could all work out for the best. Why don't you sit down at your computer and give me a few treatments. We'll do lunch at Le Dome."

They hung up, and Jonathan shouted out to his assistant, "Put Perry Newman on the DNA list, please." DNA was club jargon for "Do not admit." For Perry, Jonathan Scott would be forever unavailable.

Perry called Tim and told him the story. "Your friend Simon is right. They eat us lower L.A. boys alive in upper Los Angeles," said Perry. "Both romantically and professionally."

Tim had barely gotten used to his brother's success; now he had to deal with his brother's unemployment. This would throw the family into turmoil—Ann and Syd were used to Tim being unemployed and alone, but for Perry, these were uncharted waters. If Dad threw a couple of hundred-dollar bills Perry's way, it would barely cover his Nioxin fetish. Sunday night's dinner was shaping up to be a maudlin affair, especially coming so soon after Tim's brief moment of glory on *Which Way LA?* Having to praise Perry while pitying Tim might be standard procedure for Ann and Syd, but the Newmans had just entered Bizarro World, and Tim wasn't sure any of them were ready for it. Tim knew he wasn't, and he resolved to stay home, eat Lean Cuisine, and watch *The Simpsons*. Perry needed Ann and Syd more than he did right now.

"Mom and Dad are going to go crazy, you know," said Tim.

"Here's the worst part," said Perry. "Mom will miss Nancy. She really will."

## Awash in a Sea of Hormones

**Syd was depressed.** Perry was brokenhearted and out of work. Tim hadn't even shown up for Sunday dinner. Saving the Valley from the clutches of *them* was more work and less fun than Ann had thought it would be.

Why do things like this always happen to *me?* Ann wondered, feeling the weight of it all press down on her slight shoulders. I don't know how much more of this I can take.

So it was no surprise that she had decided to accompany a small group of CUSS members to a weekend retreat at a health spa in Laguna Beach—a chance for them to shed pounds and problems, to do good for their bodies and their city, to get away from the pressures of the life in the Valley and see the challenges they faced more objectively from a quaint, arty beach town in Orange County.

"How's the food at the spa?" asked one of the women as the tiny splinter group sat in a booth at Art's Delicatessen.

"Very brown rice, very egg white and carrot juice," explained another. "Sort of early Pritikin, but it works. You leave this place feeling ten years younger. You won't believe the energy you'll have."

"What time do they make you get up?" asked another.

"There's a brisk walk along the beach at seven A.M., but you'll want to eat first."

"Do they have yoga?"

"Do they have Pilates?"

"Do they have a labyrinth? I've always wanted to try a labyrinth."

"What I really need is a deep-tissue massage."

"I just need the opportunity to be healthy," said a slightly overweight woman. "You can't get that here."

"This sounds perfect," said Ann. "This is exactly what I need right now."

They all agreed. Plans were finalized. Reservations were made on a cell phone right there in the booth.

"I'll bring a bottle of scotch," piped up one woman. "Who wants to bring the vodka?"

The chubby woman raised her hand.

Gentiles, thought Ann, who drank only at the occasional party. I'll never understand them.

Ann thought about the woman packing their liquor as she readied her own suitcase for the big weekend. Let them pack all the booze they want, she thought. Ann had SAM-e, which *Newsweek* said good things about, but she was unsure she was feeling any mood-elevating effects. There was also her Premarin—she couldn't forget her hormone-replacement therapy for menopause. Ann was never sure if hormone replacement was a good idea. As best as she could tell, most of her problems came from hormones. Perhaps she'd better off without them. She could be so happy one day and so miserable the next, even though nothing around her had changed. That just had to be hormones. Once, years ago, during her real-estate incarnation, she'd had PMS so badly, she had rejected an offer on a house without telling the owner. A better offer came along, so it was no big problem. Another time, she bought an ugly sofa—and was never sure why. It caused her to wonder whenever she made a big decision: Which part of my body is doing the deciding? And which part is smarter?

Her other major concern was sleep. She never slept well away from Syd, so she decided to unplug the Brookstone sound machine from next to her bed and take it with her. She had gotten used to the sounds of artificial surf emanating from a microchip—although the babbling brook sound was nice also—and she thought the familiarity of her own machine would help in Laguna. Of course, there would be the sound of the live ocean right outside her window, but nature is so unpredictable. Sometimes nature is too loud and sometimes it's too soft. Brookstone had thoughtfully included a volume control.

Sleep was only one of Ann's problems. Syd was another. Syd tended to be a bit lost when left to his own devices. He could kill an afternoon or evening easily enough, but a weekend was formidable. She decided to alert the boys.

It was easier to reach Tim these days. He was usually at the office. Perry, at loose ends, was sometimes at his apartment but sometimes not. He'd go to the gym, to the mall, to Borders. Or maybe he just wasn't answering his phone.

"I'll only be gone two nights," she told Tim. "And you know how your father is."

"He's not the most self-reliant man I've ever met," acknowledged Tim. "He really needs a hobby."

"Don't I know it," said Ann, shaking her head. "Why can't I be a golf widow like every other woman my age?"

"I'll ask him if he wants to go to a movie or something," suggested Tim. "I'll try to get him out of the house."

"You're a wonderful son," said Ann. "I love you, and I'll call you when I get back."

As she feared, she was only able to get Perry's voice mail. She left a message, trying to sound upbeat. But she was worried. Tim was used to picking himself up off the floor, dusting himself off, and trying again. He's like me that way, Ann realized. Perry is more like Syd. They haven't had much experience with adversity or change. Maybe Perry had great coping skills, and Ann just didn't know it because he hadn't had to use them before. Or maybe this setback would throw him, and it would take him a long time to recover.

Ann couldn't shake that bad feeling. If I don't feel any better, she thought, I can always pretend to be a Gentile and get loaded on scotch or vodka.

# Life Without Golf

**Friday night was bound** to be the hardest. It was a terrible night for TV and it was also a night Ann and Syd would usually go out, if not with others, at least to have some dinner and maybe see a movie. Not this Friday. With Ann in Laguna Beach, Syd was a bachelor guy. Every time he caught a glimpse of himself as a bachelor guy, he was very glad he had gotten married.

Like many men his age, Syd had no friends. He never talked on the phone with a friend. He never went to a movie with a friend. Even his lunches tended to be with other guys at work—he liked them well enough, but they were employees, not real friends. Syd had a clear view of his funeral. Ann would find him six pallbearers, but they'd be the husbands of *her* friends. Syd had already served in that capacity for Seymour Gralla, the late husband of one of Ann's good friends. Six men had carried the casket, linked not by any real relationship to the body inside, but, through their wives, to the widow who followed behind.

In a life without golf, this could easily happen. Syd knew he needed a hobby. It wasn't as if he wasn't interested: So many things sounded good. Travel, cooking, gardening—even golf. But there was work and there was family, and somehow there didn't seem to be much time left over.

"Hey, lonely guy." It was Tim on the other end of the phone. "Are you lost without someone to tell you what to do?"

"A bit," said Syd. "It's always an adjustment."

"Well, I'm a lonely guy tonight, too. Want to grab a bite and see a movie? I'm a workingman now, so I can pay—as long as you order pizza."

Not that Syd would ever have questioned Tim's good heart, but this invite had Ann's fingerprints all over it. However, Syd was not in a position to be choosy. They agreed it was probably too late to do dinner and a movie, and decreed that food was probably more important.

"My side of the hill or yours?" asked Tim.

There was a long pause. Syd didn't want to make Tim drive all the way to the Valley, but . . .

"Your silence tells me that you want me to come there." Tim laughed. "And I'll do it, because now you'll feel so guilty that you'll pay."

"Should we include your brother?" asked Syd.

"I called him and left word, but he's not at his most communicative since the roof fell in on him. He leaves messages during the day on my home machine and then calls my work voice mail at night, so I figure he's avoiding actual conversation. But he's alive and all."

"I'll give him a call. See you at Casa Vega at eight-thirty?"

"Sounds good to me," said Tim.

Syd left a message for Perry, but by the time he returned home around ten, there was still no callback. No sooner had Syd settled in to watch *20/20* than the phone rang.

"What am I doing here?" It was Ann.

"You're clearing your arteries and saving the Valley from minorities," said Syd.

"I don't know why I said yes to this," said an indignant Ann. "I barely know these women. And they drink."

"At a health spa? Since when is there liquor at a spa?"

"They smuggled it in. It's like college, but with hot flashes."

"Aren't you having any fun at all?"

"Oh, I don't know. I don't know why I do these things. It sounded good at the time, but now I look around and I see this as perfectly good weekend that I'll never get back."

"Maybe you'll have a better time tomorrow. You'll do yoga; you'll get a massage. . . ."

"I don't want to do yoga and I don't want a massage. I just want to figure out why I do these things without thinking."

To Syd, Ann was always doing things and then wondering why. That horrendous couch, for instance. Syd simply assumed her hormones were running amuck.

"I had dinner with Tim. I figure you had a hand in that."

"I don't know what you're talking about. Did he have anything interesting to say?"

"The usual Tim blather. He likes his new job, he's especially keen on his new boss, and he seems to have made a friend. A girl."

"Well, there's no reason to get our hopes up there," said Ann matter-of-factly.

"I know, I know. I just don't understand why he doesn't want to come out and tell us. He must know we know."

"He will eventually," counseled Ann. "Probably when he meets someone. I think it's been difficult for him because of Perry."

That night, Syd found it impossible to sleep. Something was different. Maybe it was that Ann was missing. Maybe he was worried about the boys. Finally, at 2:00 A.M., he got up and took a Valium.

It was just as he started drifting off to sleep that he realized the real problem. The room was too quiet. Goddamn Ann had taken his Brookstone sound machine again!

# How Not to Be a
# Homo Jew Mama's Boy

**Perry hated staying at** home and listening to his phone ring. He certainly didn't feel like writing. He couldn't even bring himself to read the trades—there was something about the whole industry that seemed unsavory. The closest he got to show business were his daily chats with the lord of the gym, and since both of them were spending enormous chunks of their lives at 24-Hour Fitness, those talks were becoming more frequent.

Until he started hiding out at the gym, Perry never realized how little Peter actually did. His workout routine was surprisingly sporadic. A few minutes on this machine, a few minutes on that—not really enough to turn one into a *Men's Fitness* cover boy. But you could probably drive an SUV through Peter's arteries. He played racquetball every day and read the *Los Angeles Times, The Hollywood Reporter,* and *Variety* on a stationary bike.

Perry wasn't doing much more. 24-Hour Fitness was a refuge. He didn't much care about getting buff or even prolonging his life. "With a life like mine, why would I want to live forever?" he said when Peter suggested he crank up the speed on the treadmill.

At least the gym was already paid for. Perry had plummeted from imaginary riches to actual poverty with dazzling speed. Cable game shows pay next to nothing—bank tellers make as much—and he'd get union scale for the *Dire Straights* pilot. Well, half of union scale—cowriter Nancy would get her 50 percent. Minus agent's commission, that left Perry with slightly over seven thousand dollars, which was pretty much his Visa card balance.

Even though Perry had never made big money, he had always worked steadily, landing one job after another. His steady income and clever use of credit gave him an admirable lifestyle for a twenty-six-year-old. He'd never had those long bouts of unemployment that Tim did, as Tim sulked around his apartment, trying to make sense of his life. Now it was Perry's turn to brood.

Peter was making his rounds, and Perry watched him chatting it up with two overly muscled black guys in the Pump Room. With tattoos and knit caps, they looked like gang members, the type who first got turned on to bodybuilding in the prison yard. Peter waved at Perry to join them.

"Want to play some two-on-two with these guys?" asked Peter. "Let's show them that white guys can jump."

In a blatant attempt to lure a younger crowd and make use of its infrequently used racquetball courts, 24-Hour Fitness had thrown up a backboard and net in the one of the courts and invested in a few basketballs. Perry and Tim had tested it out when the net was first installed, but Tim got discouraged at Perry's skill and quit after fifteen minutes.

Perry had nothing to lose by playing a quick game. It might even be fun. He jogged up to the front desk and got a ball. They took turns warming up. Watching these two slow-moving behemoths lumber around the court, Perry was feeling pretty damn confident.

It turns out that in basketball, like life, speed isn't everything. The last thing Perry remembered as he drove quickly to the hoop was a massive dark elbow. Things went black, and Perry would later learn that his head had hit the wood floor with a crack so loud, Peter'd thought he might be dead. Blood gushed from his flattened nose. He heard Peter warn the others away from touching him, "I wouldn't get his blood on you, guys—I know his last girlfriend, and she was a bit of a slut." The paramedics, who were used to making stops at 24-Hour Fitness to haul off the occasional elderly angina victim, were there quickly.

Thanks to a phone call from Peter, Tim was at the hospital by the time Perry was aware what was happening.

"So, you weren't getting *enough* sympathy?" Tim asked.

"My head hurts," moaned Perry.

"Gosh, I wonder why," said Tim, pulling up a chair.

"Have you talked to the doctor?" asked Perry.

"Yes, you'll live. But you have a slight concussion and they're going to do something about that broken nose."

"Well, it's not like it was my best feature," said Perry resignedly.

"Apparently, nothing is so bad that it can't get worse."

An elegant gray-haired doctor entered. "I'm Dr. Mark Lyons. I'm your plastic surgeon. We're going to go in and repair your nose shortly, but there are a few things we should talk about first."

"Shoot."

"The damage to your nose is extensive, but it's a relatively easy job to fix. Often, when people find themselves in your situation, they want to take advantage of it. As long as we're doing the reconstruction, we can re-create the nose any way you might want. Have you ever given any thought to what type of nose might look best on you?"

Perry thought for a moment. "I want his nose," he said, pointing at his brother.

The doctor looked at Tim, who was suddenly painfully aware of the prominent Newman nose that had been passed on for generations.

"Really?" asked the doctor.

"Oh, thanks a lot, Doctor," snorted Tim.

"I'm just making sure," said Dr. Lyons. "It's all a matter of personal preference. The nurse will be down to prep you in about twenty minutes. You'll be able to go home tonight, but you'll need someone to stay with you."

Tim waved his hand in a volunteer fashion.

"You owe me," said Perry.

"*I* owe *you*?" asked Tim. "I'm the one who's going to be sleeping on your couch tonight."

"But I saved you from being the ugly Newman boy. I could have gotten a new nose, a nice Kevin Bacon number, and then when people saw us, they'd say, 'Oh, look, the twins. The cute one and Tim.' "

"I think people already say that."

"You don't get to feel sorry for yourself today, Timmy. Today is my day for self-pity. You just stand there and say, 'Thank you, dear brother, for not leaving me with the biggest nose in the family.' "

"Thank you for not leaving me with the biggest nose in the family," said Tim, "which, in our family, would be saying a lot."

"You're welcome."

"Are you sure you don't want to reconsider?"

"I can't have a nose job. I can't have people *thinking* I had a nose job. It's just too . . ." Perry was stumped for the right word.

"Too homo Jew mama's boy?" suggested Tim helpfully.

Perry laughed until it hurt, which didn't take long at all.

# Sandy's Rebuilding Year

**The one time she** bothered to read a sports story, Sandy Moore learned about the concept of the rebuilding year. The Dodgers, having lost their way the season before, had restaffed and reshuffled, but not much was expected of them. Why? Because it was their rebuilding year. Apparently, rebuilding takes but one season, and next season the Dodgers were destined for greatness. For now, however, everyone was satisfied with the rebuilding process.

That concept stuck with Sandy, especially now that she herself was rebuilding, restaffing, and reshuffling. Or maybe she was just taking a year off. Her life had gotten too weird—unhappy as an artist, still smarting from yet another breakup with yet another artist boyfriend, clashing with her parents, she made the conscious decision to give herself a breather. No art for one year. No dating (except nice safe gay guys) for one year. No family dinners or any other type of family function (phone calls, of course, were allowed) for one year. It was as complete a change of scenery as she could muster without leaving town.

For Sandy, *Hollywood Today* served much the same purpose as the gym did for Perry. Everyone had to be somewhere, and *Hollywood Today* was where Sandy ended up, killing time and making enough of a living to get by. Tim loved journalism, she could tell. When six o'clock rolled around, he couldn't bring himself to leave. He lingered, as if he'd fall behind on the career track if he didn't put in overtime every day. Sandy could have Julia Roberts on the phone, and when the clock turned six, she'd find an excuse to end the call and go home.

That allowed her to be genuinely happy for Tim's success. As much as she might rag him about being teacher's pet, she couldn't really feel competitive. Being at Jean's art show—even at the Bagelteria—now that made the competitive juices flow. However, that was an issue she'd deal with after the rebuilding year.

Tim loved being teacher's pet. He loved Simon James and he loved *Hollywood Today*. He loved Sandy. He had never felt so at home at a job in his life. Whatever his talents were—a nicely sarcastic writing style, a humorously jaundiced view of show business, an ability to get people to open up and sometimes say silly things—they served him well at *Hollywood Today*. Thanks to Simon, it did not go unnoticed. In a short period of time, Tim had gone from just being one of the staff to being a name singled out on the front door of the *Hollywood Today* Web site. He was a minor star in a very small galaxy, but at least he was a star.

Lunches and attention from Simon came more frequently. In some ways, it made life easier. The choice assignments, the biggest-name celebrities, and the fun stories automatically made their way to Tim's desk. There was no struggling, no trying to make some bimbo bit player in *Pacific Blue* sound interesting. The real stars knew how to give interviews, and the stories often wrote themselves. But it also made it harder. Tim was smart enough to know he had a chance at establishing himself, and he wasn't about to let that opportunity get away. Nor would he ever do anything to disappoint Simon. Tim wrote for an audience of one, and he was going to make damn sure that audience liked what it read.

So far, so good. At yet another long lunch with Simon, Tim became even happier.

"I've got two pieces of news for you, one good, the other even better," said Simon.

"First, in order to help promote the site and establish it as the premiere entertainment destination on the Web, we're going to take your work and syndicate it in two hundred newspapers across the country so that people can see what they're missing. You'll become the standard-bearer for the site, which is great for you. Of course, you'll be paid extra as well—we're not actually charging the newspapers for your articles; we're offering them free in exchange for the exposure, but I've talked to the backers and they understand that fairness is important, so you'll be paid the amount you would have gotten if we were charging."

*Me, a syndicated Hollywood columnist*, thought Tim. *And nationwide.* He fleetingly considered making a small joke about the irony of using Old Media to hype New Media, but then thought better of it.

Simon's second piece of news was even more mind-blowing. Synergistic Holdings, the new media enterprise that bankrolled *Hollywood Today,* along with several other sites, was making plans to go public. The IPO would be announced in the near future, and the money would fuel Synergistic's expansion plans, particularly in the field of e-commerce. Key employees would be allowed to buy stock at the issue price—probably around twelve dollars a share. Even in a depressed market, the chances were good that Synergistic's stock would rise and employees could make some substantial money.

Tim would be one of those key employees. It wasn't foolproof, Simon warned. As an employee, Tim would be required to hold his shares for six months. And in the stock market, anything could happen in six months. The market for Internet stocks had already gone through more ups and downs than Bruce Willis's career. Plus, Tim would have to find the initial money to buy his shares, increasing his risk, since if the stock tanked, he'd have no way of repaying the loan.

"Think of it as a lottery ticket," suggested Simon.

No way, thought Tim. This was no lottery ticket. This was a blank check. He couldn't begin to believe his good fortune.

## "We Are Hasidim— We React With Strength!"

**Sandy had never heard** of the Chabad Telethon, a revelation that surprised Tim not at all. Sandy's brain was a computer with a few loose cables. She could spark with the most inventive, insightful comments and then become totally baffled upon discovering that today was Wednesday, not Tuesday as she had thought. That's typically Sandy, thought Tim— much more of an artist than a journalist.

"This will be part of your pop culture education," suggested Tim, inviting Sandy to his apartment to watch the Chabad Telethon with him and Perry. "It's so bad, it's good. You'll see celebrities you thought were dead. You get to see Perry at his most deformed, and you'll get free pizza. This is the only time I'll invite you to my apartment. If you're not having fun, you can just leave, and I won't even make you feel guilty the next day."

Both Tim and Perry were hooked on the Chabad Telethon, a yearly event so low-rent, so riddled with gaffes and missteps that it managed to put both Jews and show business in such a ridiculous light that much of Los Angeles tuned in, for all the wrong reasons. A camera might point at an empty podium for a full minute; the audience missed the first few words every speaker said because microphones were turned on late. The right reasons, of course, were self-evident. Chabad House was a worthy cause—its drug-treatment center took the hard-core addicts and cured them instantly, inciting everlasting gratitude from ex-druggies and their families, all of whom showed up to help Rabbi Boruch Shlomo Cunin, Chabad's colorful leader, and the group raise more money.

That was fine, of course, but not nearly as entertaining as the rest of the show. For many Jews, the telethon was a guilty pleasure, an embarrassment that bordered on self-loathing. "We are Hasidim—we react with strength!" Rabbi Cunin would shout, sweat pouring from his hat and soaking his long beard. Then there was the sight of Cunin's posse, a group of long-coated, bearded, sweaty Hasidic rabbis, browbeating viewers for money and then shouting, "Let's dance" every time the tote board showed an increase.

Jerry Weintraub, a high-powered producer whose professional and personal conduct might not put him on anyone's list of righteous men, had adopted the charity years ago, and through strength of will, he'd put the first telethon on the air. Rabbi Cunin, who seemed to run Chabad with an iron fist, clashed with Jerry on every telethon, the two bickering on the air like an old married couple. Mix in Jan Murray, a comic so old that he apparently worked only this one day a year, and the result was true show business kitsch.

Murray was easily befuddled and exasperated ("What do you mean, we should go to the tote now? We just did a tote!"), the telethon seemed to take a toll on his health. Luckily, Hillside Country Club was crawling with semiretired lounge acts just like Murray's, and his place was eventually taken by equally befuddled and exasperated Friars Club members like Norm Crosby or Fyvush Finkle. The guests were not much better. Most of the celebrities who spoke were from the Dick Van Patten direct-to-video school, but occasionally—and this is what made it so addicting—someone totally unexpected would appear. One year, it was Bob Dylan, and Tim and Perry started each telethon convinced that someone equally good would show up.

One celebrity who always showed was Jon Voight. No one knew why. He was like the Chabad mascot. He was there, on-camera, dancing, sweating, wearing a prayer shawl—looking, by comparison, much younger and blonder than he should. It was Voight and his energetic, slightly demented involvement that gave the show its campy edge and had caused Perry and Tim to become totally addicted.

"Wow, you really got bashed," said Sandy, admiring Perry's bruised and bandaged nose when she arrived at Tim's small studio apartment in West Hollywood.

"This is what happens when you stand up to Crips on the basketball court," said Perry. "Or maybe they were Bloods. It's hard to remember."

Over the ten years that they had watched the telethon together, this was the first time either of them had included an outsider. Perry would have never brought Nancy, even during the good old days. It would have seemed a bit intrusive and would have put Tim into one of his funks. That it was Tim, who by nature was far less social than Perry, who broke with tradition seemed significant. This was a new, improved Tim, which came at a bad time, since Perry was feeling very much like a new, worsened Perry.

"Are you writing anything, or looking for a new job?" Sandy asked.

"I have to do something," said Perry. "Or I'll end up here on Tim's couch and we'll kill each other, or back in my old room at home, and I'll end up murdering both my parents. I'm thinking of taking something different, though, at least temporarily. I don't think I want to rush back into working on a show. I need a break."

"Be like the Dodgers," suggested Sandy. "Have a rebuilding year."

"That's the plan. I've considered rebuilding as a waiter. Or maybe a temp. Or working for my dad. Anything but show business."

Later, when Sandy got bored watching the same rabbis dance and sweat over and over again, Tim walked her to her car.

"Thanks for the pizza," she said.

"Just tell me you weren't totally bored by the telethon. Isn't it wonderfully bad?"

"I can honestly say that I've never seen anything like it. It was very funny when they sang 'Happy Birthday' to Elliott Gould. I've never heard such bad singing in my life."

"It's squirmy—that's why we love it," said Tim.

"And I'll never look at Jon Voight the same way. But now you have to let me show you my favorite bad show."

"Which is?"

"The Miss America Pageant. It's coming up, and I'll serve something better than pizza. Tell Perry he's invited, too, and that I said good luck on the job search. You can tell him he's much cuter now that he's ugly, if you're brave enough."

"It's not a question of bravery; it's meanness," said Tim. "I prefer to kick him when he's up."

# The Chat and Chew

**Simon James was old** enough to remember the days before publicists ruled the earth. His stories of covering Hollywood in the days before *People* magazine, *Entertainment Tonight*, and Tina Brown ruined it for everyone else were like stories of walking ten miles in the snow to get to the one-room schoolhouse—and about as relevant.

"I remember playing backgammon with Lucille Ball in her den," he told Tim and Sandy over lunch. "There was no publicist in the room making sure that Lucy said the right thing. Trust me, Lucy was fearless. She said what was on her mind and she didn't care what the consequences were. Do you know what the first thing out of her mouth was?"

Tim and Sandy stared blankly.

Simon dropped his voice several octaves, giving his best

throaty Lucy imitation. " 'Desi destroyed everything he touched.' And that was *before* I had asked a question. Can you imagine that happening today?"

Tim and Sandy dutifully shook their heads.

"And access. You wanted to hang around Bob Hope or Tony Curtis? You just called the publicist. They were glad to arrange it. No strings attached. Can you imagine that?"

"You make me feel like I was born fifty years too late," said Sandy cheerfully.

Simon glowered. It's one thing to be older, but to be seen as ancient by your staff was just plain painful.

"You make me feel like I was born *thirty* years too late," corrected Tim, quickly seizing the opportunity to blatantly suck up.

"Thank you, Tim," said Simon with a slight hint of exasperation. "Remind me to buy your perky friend a calculator."

"I'm doing an interview with Antonio Lopez tomorrow," said Tim. "And get this: The publicist apologized that she wouldn't be able to join us! As if I wanted her there."

"He is so cute," said Sandy. "He is so incredibly cute, you just know he's gay."

"Which would break the hearts of millions of teenage girls," pointed out Simon. "Is it a lunch interview?"

"Yup. Yet another chat and chew," said Tim.

Of the freakish minor talents to have—being the world's best yo-yo artist, say, or making balloon animals—mastering the chat and chew was one of the most profitable. Nimble yo-yo fingers might get you into the *Guinness Book of Records* or a onetime stint on the Jay Leno show, but the chat and chew could become a career. Better yet, it could be a launching pad to something better.

A chat and chew was the best access to a celebrity you could hope for anymore. It was an interview that took place over lunch, at either a swank restaurant or a hip one, depending on the image the publicist wanted her client to project. There would be no visit to the house or movie set, no talks with friends or family, no conversation whatsoever beyond what took place during the three courses of a meal (and reporters, hoping to prolong the lunch in a desperate search for material, always ordered dessert and endless cups of coffee). Many writers, faced with a balky subject, would describe in detail how and what the celeb in question ate, as if telling the reader that Ben Affleck ordered a Garden Burger were somehow important information.

Tim had become a chat-and-chew master. He was able to engage in enough successful banter with his subjects that their menu choices became unimportant. There was something in his nonthreatening manner, quick wit, and instinct for quirky questions that brought out the best in even the dumbest actor.

Sandy watched Tim with a certain amount of concern. She was never sure how starstruck he was and how much his puppylike enthusiasm for his job was motivated by his desire to meet and hang out with celebrities.

When it came to Antonio, Tim was mildly intrigued. He always thought those teen shows on the WB were aimed much more at gay guys like him than at teenage girls, although even he had to admit there was considerable psychic overlap between those two groups. And thanks to genetics and a personal trainer, Antonio was likely to be popular in both camps. Right now, he hovered on the cusp, a minor character hoping for a spin-off to call his own.

Antonio's publicist was definitely into positioning her client as young and hip. She chose Red, the Beverly Boulevard hangout for the Matts and Bens, Treys and Matts, and Tobeys and Skeets of the world. It was painted red, of course, and very casual. It was also a bit noisy, so Tim shoved his tape recorder all the way to Antonio's side of the table, figuring he'd be able to remember his own questions.

It was a painless chat and chew. Antonio was eager to please, early enough on his career curve to want to make a good impression. He tried hard, and sometimes paused, frantically searching for a witty answer. Sometimes it would come to him while he was answering the next question, and he'd quickly backtrack, verbally rewriting his previous response, hoping that Tim would forget the first answer and use the better one. He and Tim were about the same age, which made it easier, especially when Tim asked if he had played with GI Joes as a kid. They talked about toys giddily, and there was no reason for Tim to prolong the lunch by ordering dessert. Antonio seemed to be having a good-enough time that he wasn't about to rush off.

Two hours later, as they sat in an empty restaurant, Tim was done.

"So, I hear you're syndicated now," said Antonio.

"Yes, actually, you'll be the first one to be on the Web site and then get distributed to all these newspapers."

"That's pretty cool—I mean, for both of us."

"Yeah, I'm pretty excited. It's a good break for me."

"You're off the clock now, right?" asked Antonio. "The interview is over and all?"

"Oh, yes, I have some really good stuff. You were great. It'll be a great column."

Antonio looked at the floor awkwardly. "I just wanted to ask you a question."

"That's fair game," said Tim. "I asked you about a hundred."

"Gus Van Sant is sort of a friend of mine and he wants me to come by tomorrow night and watch a rough cut of this movie he's working on. I thought maybe if you were interested, you might want to come along, and afterward we could grab some dinner or just hang out."

What is wrong with this picture? wondered Tim. Even if he had had something better to do—like a slumber party with Kato Kaelin—he would have canceled it in a nanosecond to spend an evening with Antonio.

## California Pizza Kitchen Cares

**It was a warm Sunday** afternoon, and rather than sit around his apartment waiting for the dreaded call, Perry chose to get it over with.

"I figured it was my turn to pick up dinner," he said to his mother. "What's your pleasure? Koo Koo Roo? El Pollo Loco?" If only there were more chicken outlets, he wished. Or better yet, if only there was steak to go and Ann would allow beef on the table.

"I'm feeling adventurous," confided Ann. "Margaret took me to lunch at the California Pizza Kitchen on Ventura Boulevard the other day, and you know what? It was delicious. I had forgotten how good their Oriental chicken salad is. Except for the cilantro, of course. But I think everyone hates cilantro."

"You phone it in and I'll pick it up," said Perry.

"And your father will pay," added Ann.

Now that dinner was settled, Perry could ponder lunch. Usually, on a Sunday like this, he'd head over to the gym, but basketball was out of the question—one more sharp blow to the Newman nose and he'd look like an apple doll. Besides, the accident had taken the fun out of 24-Hour Fitness. That left him with limited options, which, as far as he could tell, meant either buying shoes at the Beverly Center and eating a poisonous food-court meal or wandering around Farmer's Market, where the food was better and he'd be outdoors.

Farmer's Market turned out to be a mistake. He had forgotten that wandering around the various food stalls on a Sunday was something that couples did. Tourist couples, local couples, young couples, old couples, pregnant couples, couples with kids, gay couples, couples who would stay together forever and never, ever fire each other. Real couples, in other words. Could there be anything more depressing than that?

He ordered ribs. Why not? Ann had convinced her family that beef was lethal, and suicide by baby backs seemed as good a way to go as any.

Later, when he was picking up dinner, he realized that killing himself wasn't going to be so easy, not as long as his mother was in charge of the menu. Four big salads and four pizzas—cheeseless, of course—were waiting.

"How many will be eating?" asked the cashier.

Perry held up four fingers and the cashier packed four sturdy disposable black plastic plates, four sets of shiny black utensils, and enough napkins and bread for a small party.

"Now this is dinner," said Ann as he did the unpacking. "Syd, look at this. I don't have to do anything—everything we need for a nice dinner is right here. We're going to have to use CPK more often. They know how to do this right."

Syd was usually very much in favor of anything that saved Ann additional labor—or *any* labor, for that matter. But he was lost in his own thoughts and barely acknowledged his wife's unadulterated joy.

Ann placed the pizza in the oven as they sat around the den and watched *60 Minutes* while they waited for Tim.

"Can I ask you a question?" Ann inquired earnestly.

"Sure," said Perry with a certain trepidation. There was always the risk that Mom would ask something absurdly personal and embarrass everyone in the room, including herself.

"Do you ever go *downtown*?" she asked, her voice full of mystery.

At first, Perry was mystified. Was that a sex term? She had once asked him, unexpectedly, what "around the world" meant, and he'd earnestly given her a travel-based answer. "You'd think my own son would be hipper than that," she'd said in disgust. Perry hardly wanted a repeat performance. Or did she mean downtown as in black clothing, cigarettes, and lots of attitude? What in the hell was she talking about?

"You know," she explained. "Downtown L.A, where City Hall is."

Of course! Once again, there was less than meets the eye to one of Ann's questions.

"Not much," said Perry. "Nancy and I went to an Emmy party at Cicada. That was fun. I saw the Lakers once at the Staples Center, but they lost."

Ann adopted a slightly pained expression. Clearly, she wasn't getting through.

"I mean, is it safe? Did you feel as if you were in danger?"

"At the Staples Center?" He laughed. "It's not Watts, Mom. They don't shoot you on the street, if that's what you mean."

"Your mother's secession group is going to City Hall," explained Syd, speaking for first time that evening. "She's frightened. She hasn't been downtown since *Sweeney Todd* played at the Music Center and she insisted we go to a matinee because it would be safer."

Tim arrived, carrying a small stack of newspapers.

"Mom's afraid to go downtown," Perry told him.

"Lots of minorities there, Mom," mocked Tim. "All of them armed. A nice white woman like yourself won't stand a chance." He paused. "Can I have your car when you're gone?"

"That's not funny," complained Ann.

"Besides, the car goes back to the dealership," added Syd.

Attention shifted quickly to the newspapers. Tim had just picked them up at the newsstand at Van Nuys and Ventura, which had a solid selection of out-of-state papers. Each one had his first column.

Everyone oohed and aahed, even Perry, who felt a strong twinge of resentment. Tim seemed to sense his discomfort. "Okay, you've seen them. Now I'm hungry. Where's the Koo Koo Roo?"

"I have a surprise for you," said Ann. And she unveiled the special California Pizza Kitchen feast.

"Whoa, they even give you plates," said Tim.

"They know how to serve," agreed Ann.

As they sat down, Perry spoke, using a smaller voice than he might have usually. "I have a surprise, too," he said. "I got a job."

Everyone lowered their plastic forks to the table.

"Starting tomorrow, I'm teaching English at Crosswinds. It's a sort of progressive, sort of elitist private high school in Westwood."

"What happened to TV?" asked Tim.

"I decided I needed a break," answered Perry. "Teaching's not a long-term gig."

"I didn't know you could teach," said Ann.

"It's an emergency situation. I'm replacing a teacher who was sent off to rehab. And private schools have different rules. You don't need credentials or anything. Basically, you just need to know someone, and I did."

"Crosswinds?" said a distracted Syd, shaking his head. "Crosswinds? I've never heard of it."

"Get with it, Dad," said Tim. "It's been in *Vanity Fair*. It's where stars send their kids. Right, Perry?"

"A lot of stars," agreed Perry. "A lot of money. As I understand it, I'll be surrounded by a bunch of well-to-do, spoiled Jewish kids."

"That's what we were," pointed out Tim. "You'll fit in just fine."

Tim left almost immediately after dinner. Perry lingered, watching *Who Wants to Be a Millionaire* with his parents.

When it was time to head home, Syd got out his wallet. "How much was dinner?" he asked.

"Forty bucks, give or take," said Perry.

"You've never really had to dress up for work, have you?" asked Syd, seeming to focus on the conversation for the first time since Perry arrived. "You've always been able to dress casually. I suppose you'll be buying some nicer clothes for your new job." He peeled off several bills, well beyond the forty he owed Perry.

"Not at this school, Dad. It's a jeans and sneakers kind of place. I already have the perfect wardrobe."

"Are you sure?"

Perry took two twenties. "Thanks, Dad. If the money situation goes south, you'll be the first to know."

# We Have Met the Enemy...and He Dresses Nicely

**Ann slept little the** night before she and the other members of CUSS were due in downtown Los Angeles. It was silly; she knew that. She'd been to New York and survived. But New York was a real city, and Los Angeles was something completely different. Everybody lived, worked, and played in Manhattan, except during August. In L.A., everyone was so spread out. There was no center to the dozens of unique areas that made up Los Angeles, and that's why Ann hated downtown L.A. so much. It was a big mean poseur. It merely pretended to be the center. It demanded attention. It insisted on having the Staples Center and the Convention Center, both of which could have gone just about anywhere. You could have put the Music Center in any other part of the city—the Valley, say—and it would have been much more practical. Would the power brokers who ran L.A. have allowed that? Hardly. Even the Cathedral of Our Lady of the Angels, the multimillion-dollar Catholic superchurch meant to replace the earthquake-damaged St. Vibiana's, would be located downtown, too, financed by the same power brokers who seemed oblivious to the fact that most people in L.A. were just like Ann and wouldn't step foot in downtown Los Angeles unless heavily armed with pepper spray.

Downtown hadn't always been so superfluous in Ann's mind. She could remember that as a young girl, growing up in Santa Monica, downtown had had a role. Before L.A. began to accept its fate of forty free-floating suburbs, the city was built on the same model as other American cities. Downtown was the center, and the rest of the areas were insignificant satellites. The big department store chains had gigantic main stores in downtown L.A., floors upon floors of clothes, furniture, and appliances. The suburban stores were tiny, and the staff was constantly calling the main store to see if some special mattress was in stock. If you had a big purchase or wanted to get your Christmas shopping out of the way, you piled into the old Buick and took Olympic Boulevard downtown to a big store, where you could get everything done.

Eventually, everyone got smart. Downtown was ugly, dirty, and inconvenient. The big stores closed down. The satellite stores went to where the customers were, grew bigger, and anchored nice malls, where sensible people shopped. Even the stodgy lawyers and accountants, who, like their eastern brethren, assumed that downtown was the place to be, figured out that it was better to be near their clients than close to government offices, and they moved to West L.A. or Century City. Downtown Los Angeles was never very much of a vibrant place, and as time went on, it grew less and less relevant. You could see a play or a basketball game. You could serve jury duty. You could go to the Museum of Contemporary Art. You could go to City Hall. You could step over countless homeless guys sleeping on the sidewalk. But that was about all downtown had to offer.

"Know thy enemy," advised Linda, the CUSS leader. That's why the brave little group of CUSS members were downtown, walking through the metal detectors at City Hall, making their way to the drafty city council chambers to watch the bloated, power-hungry city council in action. The city council and the mayor would do everything in their power to stop L.A. from splitting in two, and if CUSS was going to beat them, it had better get a sense of who and what they were.

What L.A. really needs is a good-looking, well-dressed politician, thought Ann, watching the city council in action. She'd never seen a larger group of fashion-impaired red-meat eaters in her life. Even the women tipped the scales at two hundred-plus-pounds. And those clothes! Where did they find clothes that were so . . . boxy and unappealing? Probably downtown, Ann concluded.

"Who wants to have lunch?" asked Linda as they left the city council members to drone on about zoning matters none of them understood. "I was thinking of Cicada."

Ann had originally thought that she'd drive straight home, thanking God that she had not been mugged, lost, or even offended by the unpleasant odors she assumed permeated downtown. But Perry had said good things about Cicada, and she was intrigued. If it was good enough for an Emmy party . . .

Forget about the nearly perfect Italian food the members of CUSS had for lunch. It was the building that astounded Ann. An Art Deco masterpiece built during downtown's golden era. It was simply gorgeous, and it made Ann yearn for an elegance she remembered from years ago, when her mother would take her to the tearoom at Bullock's Wilshire and she'd wear gloves because it was such a special event. At Cicada, the men—and the customers were mostly men—wore business suits. Older men in suits. Young men in suits. Even the few women were smartly dressed. Ann liked that.

It was hard to think about driving home after such a large meal, and if you were really going to get to know your enemy, it seemed like a good idea for everyone to walk around downtown a bit. After all, there's safety in numbers. Would marauding gangs of young hooligans actually attack six women in broad daylight on the crowded streets?

What started out as espionage against the forces of darkness somehow turned into an architectural walking tour. The Bradbury Building, the oldest commercial building in L.A., with its intuitive combination of Mexican tile, Belgian marble, and intricate wrought iron, not to mention its five-story skylight, actually gave Ann chills. The Biltmore Hotel's hand-painted lobby ceiling hadn't changed from her childhood visits. And Bunker Hill was nicely developed now—its highrise apartments seemed so cosmopolitan and New Yorkish, with their views of the downtown skyline. Even Angel's Flight, the little cable car that took you to the top of Bunker Hill and gave you the best view of all, was back. It had been one of Ann's favorite things to do downtown when she was little, and then it had been torn down. Now rebuilt and cleaner, it still only charged a quarter.

"Let's do something really daring," suggested Linda. The next thing she knew, Ann was in a subway station under downtown, taking the Red Line. It was even cleaner than Angel's Flight, and better yet, it worked on the honor system. No turnstiles, no tokens—you simply slipped a dollar bill in an ATM-like machine. It ran only five miles, and ran them quickly. Nervous, the CUSS members got out on the last stop and didn't even venture up to ground level. They simply reboarded the train and rode quietly back to downtown. Suddenly, everything in the Valley seemed so new and characterless. Ann loved the energy level downtown. It was so exciting, it was almost like being in Las Vegas.

Ann was still thrilled when Syd got home for dinner. "We must go to a Lakers game," gushed Ann. "I hear the Staples Center is wonderful and that there are lots of good places to eat nearby. We can make a night of it."

That sounded good to Syd, who nodded and ate more of the Johnnie's pizza that had just been delivered.

"And you know something else?" whispered Ann. "I think I might like to try living downtown. I was thinking that when you retire, we could get an apartment at Bunker Hill. It would be so sophisticated."

"We'll have to go down and look around," said Syd agreeably. He knew that Ann's desire to live in a high rise would soon pass, but he couldn't help but wonder how soon she'd be looking for a new project to replace CUSS to fill her days.

## Getting in Touch with Your Inner Teenage Girl

**"I need the style doctor,"** said Tim as he looked down into Sandy's cubicle.

"You need a style *hospital*," joked Sandy, "and even then, you'd only begin to catch up."

"I'm gay. I'm no stranger to sarcasm," said Tim. "Do you want to help or not?"

"What's the occasion? Movie premiere? Club opening? Book signing?"

"Worse." Tim frowned. "A date."

Sandy was floored. In their four months as cell mates, Tim had never once mentioned another man. He was one of those harmless asexual gay guys, which made him seem like better friend fodder. Sandy wasn't so sure about those randier homosexuals—she'd never understood one-night stands, sex in a rest room, or dressing up like a rodeo cowboy.

"A date? As in a date with a guy?"

"I'm afraid so," admitted Tim.

Sandy blamed herself. It was that Century City makeover. She had created a monster. A sex monster. And that was no good at all. One of the best things about Tim's eunuchlike quality was that it made her feel better about her own spinster life. They could sit around, eat pizza, and not talk about boys together. But if Tim was going to date, then he'd feel compelled to talk about it. Ick, thought Sandy. Girl talk with a gay guy. She knew that inside even the straightest gay man is a teenage girl just dying to talk about how "dreamy" Mr. Right is.

"Aren't you out of shape for this?" she asked.

"I told you, I go to the gym," Tim said defensively. "I'm not overweight; I just don't seem to form muscles."

"I didn't mean that type of shape," she said impatiently. "I meant emotionally. Hasn't it been awhile since you've dated?"

That was true enough. Tim had entered a virtual monastery shortly after he grew pubic hair, and he had stayed there ever since. Sure, he had strayed a handful of times. Sex with his college roommate exactly five times, until his roommate remembered he was a heterosexual and gave Tim the cold shoulder. Then there was that post–college period, when Tim forced himself to have casual sex with strange men he'd meet in bars. But once he realized that each and every time he did it, it made him miserable, he gave it up. He'd known he couldn't live his life this way forever—loneliness can drive you crazy, after all—but he'd figured he'd get around to fixing it eventually, maybe after he solved that pesky career problem.

"I just want to look nice, and I don't trust myself enough to pick out my own clothes."

Sandy—always the bridesmaid, even to her male friends—momentarily imagined choosing a hideous ensemble, one that would make Tim look like a sportscaster. But her better instincts took over and she agreed to help.

"Who's the lucky fellow?" she asked as they drove to Tim's apartment.

"Antonio," said Tim somewhat sheepishly.

It was as if Sandy had been roused from a deep sleep: "You can't date someone you're writing about! You know that. You went to journalism school. Even I know that, and I've never even seen *All the President's Men.*"

"I'm pathetic," admitted Tim. "I couldn't say no. Besides, I'm not sure it's even a date. He never said the word *date.* I never said it. Maybe it's just two guys having dinner and seeing a movie."

Here's what Sandy wanted to say: You idiot. Don't you realize he's flattering you just so you'll write great stuff about him? Once again, she succumbed to her kinder, gentler side.

"I suppose it's all right. You deserve something wonderful."

"I've already gotten the column, so I'm feeling well satisfied in the 'wonderful' department," said Tim. "It's been so long since anyone asked me out, I was too stunned to think. He's certainly the best-looking guy I'll ever date, even if it's just this once."

"He is *amazing*-looking," agreed Sandy. "I'm assuming he's dumber than a log."

"I wouldn't want him to take my SAT for me," said Tim. "It's just a night out."

"Men." Sandy sighed. "You're so superficial. Looks are the only thing that counts."

"And you wouldn't do the same thing?" Tim asked.

Well, maybe, thought Sandy. But it would snow in Santa Monica before she'd give Tim *that* satisfaction.

Seeing Tim's apartment reminded Sandy how humbly he lived. She'd noticed it the night of the Chabad Telethon, but now the thought of Tim possibly bringing Antonio Lopez to his one-room apartment on an alley, with a kitchen straight out of a trailer and a bathroom with a grungy shower and no tub, made Sandy feel sympathy. Tim didn't even have a bed, for God's sake. Just a big futon on a collapsible wooden frame that doubled as a couch. He was lucky to have a color TV.

"I do very good work," said Sandy as she assembled clothes from their earlier shopping spree. "You'll look very presentable."

"I can't ask for more than that," said Tim.

He drove her back to her car on his way to Antonio's. "Maybe we shouldn't mention this to Simon," he said plaintively. "He's sorta old school."

"My lips are Velcroed," agreed Sandy.

"Is it okay if I call you when I get home tonight?" asked Tim as he dropped her off.

Arrrgh. How *Tiger Beat.* How *Jane.* How *Sassy.* Sandy wasn't sure she was ready to listen to the sounds of Tim in love. On the other hand, it's not as if she'd be doing anything more interesting.

"Don't call too late," she said. "It's a school night."

"I won't," said Tim. "I promise." He pulled away in his dusty Honda Civic, nervous and happy and worrying about sweat stains.

# Vive l'Indépendance

**Private schools never call** themselves private schools. That would be a tad too snobbish, and while snobbishness is the foundation of their very existence, it would be much too revealing to admit it. That's why they're called independent schools. It captures the very essence of the pioneer spirit that drives parents to shell out seventeen thousand dollars a year to keep their children out of the dependent (or is it nonindependent?) public schools. It would be easier to make fun of L.A.'s network of private schools were the public school system not so dismal. How bad are the schools in L.A.? Put it this way: were it not for social promotion, no one would graduate at all and the kindergarten population alone would be the seventh-largest country in the world.

Still, Perry had mixed feelings about Crosswinds. But he liked its reputation as progressive school. Some of the other independent schools, like Harvard-Westlake and Brentwood, were stifling in their stuffiness. Brentwood often gave detention to snuff out any creativity before it reached critical mass.

But Crosswinds was a virtual utopia of creativity, a liberal experiment gone right, a sea of children allowed to express themselves while learning. That was the good news. The bad news was that it was a rich utopia. The student phone directory was worth five hundred dollars to any good tabloid reporter, since it contained the unlisted numbers of so many stars and studio executives. They were generous parents, too. How many high schools have a planetarium?

How different are the rich? They're different in obvious ways—Perry had already heard jokes about the student parking lot, and indeed, it looked like a convention of new SUV owners. They're different in little ways, too. One teacher gleefully showed him the car pool list. Due to the enormous percentage of kids living under joint-custody arrangements, alternately spending three days with Dad and four with Mom one week, and then switching to four and three the next, scheduling car pools took the skills of an air-traffic controller. Some parents used Excel to keep it straight, and even then carpooling was so complicated that everyone was relieved when their children turned sixteen and could drive themselves.

Perry thought about Tim as he walked across the high school campus. This campus was called the upper campus. A few blocks away, there was the elementary school, the lower campus. But since this was Crosswinds, it was all, to use Tim's favorite term, very upper L.A. That made this the upper upper campus, and the elementary school the upper lower campus. Tim would like that.

Perry was taking over an English class vacated when the regular teacher fell asleep in her own class, often before the students did. Interestingly, the school knew the teacher had a drug problem when they hired her. It was part of Crosswinds' enlightened philosophy—giving people a second chance, being open-minded about their flaws and idiosyncrasies. But even at Crosswinds, passing out in class was not allowed—nor were teachers encouraged to take more drugs than their students—and that's what she had done. Perry was a long-term substitute, but only a substitute. The other teacher would return, and Crosswinds was quite proud of that. What better lesson could it teach its students than to show how someone could triumph over adversity?

"You'll want to address the issue in each of your classes," suggested Bob Parrish, the earnest upper school's director. "We don't want to keep secrets from our community members. Encourage them to talk about it. I think you'll be surprised how accepting they are."

Perry decided to try it. As he stood awkwardly before his first-period English class for tenth graders, he wrote his name on the white board with a marker.

"I'm Perry Newman," he said. Before he could continue, the class chanted back, "Hi, Perry," as if they were in an AA meeting.

Undaunted, Perry went on. "I'll be filling in for Toni Scheer while she recuperates—"

The class laughed loudly. "We know where she is," said one student.

"Okay," Perry said, correcting himself, "while she's in rehab."

"Do you know if she's at Promises in Malibu?" asked Caitlin, the girl with the pierced eyebrow. "That would be so cool, because that's where my older brother is right now."

"Promises rocks," agreed Alex, while the class nodded. Alex was wearing shoes he had fashioned from duct tape. As he had explained before school, he was testing them. If they lasted through the day, he'd think about marketing them at Urban Outfitters on the Santa Monica Promenade. He knew they'd sell like crazy, if he could just prove they were practical.

"What happened to your nose, Perry?" asked a student in regular shoes.

"I broke it playing basketball." There were murmurs of approval throughout the class.

"Did you get your nose done, as long as you were there?" asked Caitlin.

"I decided to stick with my original nose," answered Perry, and the murmurs of approval stopped.

"Well, at least you have nice hair," offered Caitlin as something of a consolation prize. Any flattering comment about his hair invigorated Perry. It helped him justify the hundreds of dollars he spent on hair-care products.

"I understand all the tenth-grade classes are reading *To Kill a Mockingbird,*" said Perry, "but that every class moves at its own pace. Can anyone give me a sense of how far along you guys are?"

"I can," said Alex. He took out a weathered yellow-and-black Cliffs Notes version of *To Kill a Mockingbird* and opened it to page ten. Holding it aloft, he said, "We're right here."

Perry knew exactly what that meant. In his briefcase under the desk, he had his own Cliffs Notes. He thought it might give him an edge with the smarter students.

"Okay, I think I know what you're talking about," said Perry. "Is everyone pretty much in the same place?"

"Not me," said Caitlin mournfully. "My mother had a face peel that went very, very badly, so I haven't been able to do any reading at all."

## Vive la Différence

**"You didn't call last night,"** said Sandy when Tim wandered in a full hour late to work.

"I didn't go home last night," answered Tim.

"Oh," said Sandy disapprovingly. "Now I'm sorry I brought it up."

"A little too quick, first date and all?" asked Tim sheepishly.

"It's just different for you, I guess."

"Do you want to hear my favorite gay joke?" asked Tim.

Sandy nodded.

"What does a lesbian bring to her second date?"

Sandy shrugged.

"A U-Haul. And what does a gay guy bring to his second date?"

"I don't know."

"What second date?" Tim laughed aloud, having amused himself greatly.

"I don't get it."

Tim sighed. "Lesbians are big on commitment. They fall in love and form relationships very quickly. We gay guys are flighty and promiscuous. We see a guy once and move on."

"I thought you were different."

"I was different," said Tim. "Until last night, I was very different. But being different wasn't working for me."

"And this is working for you?"

"I don't know, but I'm giving it a try."

"So tell me about it," said Sandy reluctantly. "But if you give me one slimy sexual detail, I'll put my hands over my ears and scream and attract a crowd."

Poor Tim. His main memories of the night before were slimy and sexual and, frankly, it had been so long and it had gone so well that he really wanted to talk about it. Sex with a TV star? Isn't bragging one of the best parts? Especially after such a lengthy sex drought? He would never tell Sandy, but if Antonio had been a good-looking cable guy, Tim's desperation would still have caused him to throw himself at his feet.

"Okay," Tim began hesitantly. "He's very nice, he really is. He asks a lot of questions, but I'm not sure if he's asking them because he cares or because he fears he's self-absorbed and he's trying to throw me off the track. I'm giving him the benefit of the doubt on that one. And he has that weird actor thing, where he's sort of shy—I mean, genuinely shy—but he really likes the fact that people in the restaurant are looking at him."

"If he didn't like people looking at him, he'd be in the wrong profession," said Sandy.

"True enough. And he's very flattering, but in a passive-aggressive way."

"How so?"

"Like my car. He didn't want to say he wasn't impressed by a Honda Civic, so he said, 'I really saw you as more of the BMW type.' Which is sort of a nice thing to say, but also not so nice, since I'm driving the Civic."

"I love your Civic," said Sandy.

"I don't much love it," said Tim. "And I suppose it would be stupid to expect him to love it."

"Did you talk about the article?"

"We joked about it, mostly. About how he was really at my mercy now, that I could write the story that could destroy his career. Plus, I know about the tattoo—"

Sandy held up her hand. "Stop," she said. "You're not going there."

Tim laughed. He *had been* going there, but now he couldn't.

"He said he probably wouldn't read it, that it would be too weird. And it's going to be plenty weird to write, too."

He handed her Antonio's press kit, full of adoring glamour shots of the great Antonio Lopez.

"Do you know what you're going to say?"

"I don't have a clue. I don't have an angle; I don't have a lead. I have nothing. I've never felt so blocked in my life."

Sandy glanced at the deadline schedule pinned to her cubicle wall.

"Lucky you," she said. "It's due today."

Tim formed his hand in the shape of a gun, placed his finger to his temple, and pulled the trigger. "Bang," he said.

"Do you actually believe that he won't read it?" asked Sandy. "I'd be dying to read it if I were him."

"I don't think he reads much, period. And I'm not sure he thinks too highly of journalists."

"What makes you say that?"

"Just something he said. He said that I seemed very smart. In fact, he thought I was so smart that he couldn't figure out why I didn't write screenplays."

"Oh, yes, it *is* a higher art form."

"Well, at least it's one he understands."

"So what did you say?"

"I didn't know what to say, because he was offering it as a compliment. And there's part of me that would like him to be right." There's also the fact that Tim was just plain needy. Tim knew that. So did Sandy, but neither mentioned it.

Sandy started giggling.

"Why are you laughing?" asked Tim, hurt.

"I just got it. I just got your joke."

"You are way slow. I wouldn't even admit that if I were you."

"No, it's funny. Second dates. I get it now. Do you think you two will have a second date?"

"We're supposed to. Tonight."

"So I guess you'll be late again tomorrow."

Tim laughed. "I don't want to push my luck with Simon. Anyway, I could have gotten here on time. I was up early—I don't sleep all that well in strange places—but I went to the gym."

"Gosh, I wonder why," said Sandy, looking at the press kit photos.

"Exactly," agreed Tim.

# Turkish Prison Looks Good to Syd

**It was shaping up** to be the worst day in Syd Newman's life. This morning, as he sat reading the paper, Ann had uttered the most dreaded sentence possible: "Syd, I was thinking we should have a party."

Syd was not happy. Given the choice between throwing a party and spending a week in a Turkish prison, Syd would have to flip a coin. He longed for the days before the boys left home, when Ann didn't need so many projects. Now, with CUSS behind her, Ann was floundering, looking to fill those extra five hours a week that she usually dedicated to her career or a cause. Throwing a party was a perfect bridge between CUSS and whatever would come next.

Things are never so bad that they can't get worse. "Guess

who wants to see you for lunch?" asked Gladys when he arrived at work. "Sam Donaldson and his news team."

"Sam Donaldson" was Dr. Brian DeSalvo, the unofficial leader of the small group of partners Syd had assembled twenty years earlier to buy the dealership. He was a Valley dentist with a very bad hairpiece, apparently purchased from the same mail-order firm patronized by the legendary Sam Donaldson himself. More than anything, Dr. DeSalvo fancied himself a businessman. The idea that DeSalvo had assembled the partners for lunch, without talking to Syd first, could only be bad news.

A party at home. An insurrection among his partners at work. Syd wished he had a hobby that might distract him, but something would probably go wrong there, too.

"We're having a party, Gladys." Syd sighed.

"I'm sorry," said Gladys sincerely. "I really am."

"Bad things happen," said Syd philosophically. "There's nothing we can do about it."

It didn't take long for Ann to slip into her obsessive-compulsive gear.

Telephone call number one (at 10:17 A.M.): "It's beautiful this time of year. I think we should do it in the backyard, but catered—nothing too fancy, but something nice. And music. We should have live music."

Telephone call number two (10:53 A.M.): "Linda knows a wonderful restaurant on the beach in Malibu where her gynecologist's cousin was married. She thinks it would be perfect for our party. Is it too expensive? Or should I find out how much it costs first?"

Telephone call number three (11:20 A.M.): "Chris and Sarah went to a wonderful party on a boat in the marina. It cruises around the marina, but never really goes out to sea, so no one gets seasick. Sarah called it 'the booze cruise.' What do you think? That's not us, is it?"

Telephone call number four (11:50 A.M.): "In case you're looking for me, Linda and I are going to Malibu to check out that restaurant. It sounds just perfect."

Lunch went badly. Too many forced smiles, too much bad news.

"I'm sure you understand our position," said Dr. DeSalvo, a smarmy grin permanently affixed across his artificially tanned face. "We all have a good deal of our personal and retirement savings invested in the dealership. And we all appreciate what you've done. We've had safety and a steady return on our investment."

"You're welcome," said Syd wanly.

"But times have changed. We feel we can get a better return, and let's face it, you can't retire without six mil in the bank anymore. And none of us are getting any younger." There were nods all around.

"I can't buy you out, if that's what you're suggesting," said Syd. "I don't have access to that type of money."

"We don't expect you to," said DeSalvo. "We have an interested party already. Actually, I have an interested party. It's, shall we say, an unconventional proposal, and I'd really love to tell you more, but I've signed a confidentiality agreement. If it makes you feel any better Syd, no one at this table knows more than you—except me, of course. I just wanted to get everyone on board and ask them to have an open mind."

"When will we see this mystery proposal?" asked Syd. "And do they intend to buy all of us out, or just you guys?"

"We're all taken care of." The dentist smiled. "Of course, they want to meet with you and explain their plans. Perhaps you two will connect."

"And if we don't?"

"This is no ordinary deal. We'll all be getting stock in a most exciting venture. I want to say more, but I can't. Trust me."

"I can't live on stock," said Syd. "This isn't merely an investment for me; it's my livelihood."

"Trust me," DeSalvo said again, flashing his capped teeth. "Trust me."

Telephone call number five (2:22 P.M.): "What a dump. I've never been so disappointed in my life. Why are all the restaurants in Malibu so run-down? And why do they smell so bad? Linda said there was no way she'd even allow us to have our party in such an awful place."

Back at his office, Syd pondered his uncertain future. He prided himself on being a realistic man. He knew what Newman's Super Honda was worth on the open market, and frankly, the times being what they were, it didn't make sense to sell. It made sense to hold on, rake in the profits, and wait. Why was DeSalvo so intent on selling at the bottom of the market? And what was this mysterious stock swap that had him so excited?

Telephone call number six (3:01 P.M.): "Is a hotel banquet room too stuffy? Is that too wedding receptionish?"

Syd went on-line to Amazon.com. He'd heard about these golf videotapes that could improve anyone's game by six or seven strokes. Syd didn't have a game to improve, as such—he hadn't stepped foot on a golf course in fifteen years—but it might not hurt to buy the whole set. Watching them might just get him in the mood to buy some clubs and take up golf, like every other man his age.

Telephone call number seven (4:09 P.M.): "Now Linda thinks a bowling alley would be fun, in a campy way. You know, we could have shirts made and give out trophies. But I'm not sure my back is up to it. I'll call you later."

Telephone call number eight (5:25 P.M.): "I just had the best idea. It's such a beautiful time of year. What would you think if we did it in our own backyard? We'd cater it, of course, but keep it very casual. We could even have live music. Isn't that a great idea?"

## Perry Cleans Up

**There are many wonderful** things money can buy, but probably the best is fluff-and-fold laundry. Perry hadn't made a fortune at *Boing!* But he had made enough—and been busy enough—to fall into the weekly habit of dropping his laundry off at Flair Cleaners on Saturday and picking it up Tuesday after work, with his shirts nicely starched on hangers and the rest of his laundry neatly folded and wrapped in blue paper. Fluff-and-fold was a given in Perry's life—an indulgence, sure, but one that he deserved.

Or used to deserve. The new Perry had a humbler, down-sized existence. Perhaps the most concrete example of that was in his hand right now. A miniature box of Tide, purchased, at a premium, from a vending machine. Perry was about to embark on doing his own laundry in a coin-op Laundromat.

He had his quarters. He had his tiny box of Tide. He had two adjoining machines—one for colors, one for whites. All he needed was Prozac. Or heroin. Anything to make him forget that he had now fallen to the lowest of lows.

Doing laundry didn't scare him much. But as he looked at his collection of J. Crew cotton button-down shirts, he became extremely frightened. Cleaning a shirt is one thing. Folding it is another. He'd never quite mastered folding, but he could fake it. Ironing was another, bigger challenge. He had never ironed before. Nor, for that matter, did he own an iron. He wasn't even sure where you could buy them.

He recalled a conversation he'd had with Tim years ago. Was it years ago? Maybe, given the speed of his descent, it had been only months ago. Perhaps weeks ago. So much had happened, it was hard to remember. He had chided Tim for his one-note wardrobe of jeans and T-shirts. "Don't you own a real shirt?" he asked Tim, who seemed permanently clothed in Old Navy pocket tees. "What do you wear on job interviews?"

"Oh, I have a job interview shirt," said a chipper Tim. "But it's such a pain in the ass to iron it that I save it for very special occasions."

Of course, the last time he'd seen Tim was postmakeover. Sandy had added just a touch of *GQ* to Tim's closet. The pocket tees were gone, and Perry couldn't imagine Tim, the least dexterous person below the age of ninety in Los Angeles, doing the work necessary to maintain that crisp new look. That meant that Tim was getting his laundry professionally done. And Perry was in the coin-op, clutching his Tide.

It didn't bother Perry that Tim was finally finding some success. What bothered him was Tim's attitude. It wasn't open arrogance—Tim was never openly *anything*. But Perry could tell. He could sense a certain cockiness. It wasn't just that Tim was suddenly making money, either. Tim was getting off on Perry's misfortune. That's what was irksome. Not that Tim had said anything—that would be very unlike Tim. But Tim wasn't fooling Perry, not for a second. Tim was flaunting his own success while basking in Perry's failure. And he was being much too subtle about it for Perry to call him on it.

Perry put half the box of Tide in one washing machine and half in the other. He shoved his quarters in and found a chair near a stack of old magazines. He picked up a *Newsweek*, but the cover story on the Internet only made him think of Tim's success. The *Us* magazine reminded him of Tim's syndicated column. That left *Reader's Digest*, a magazine he hadn't read since his one and only physical exam when he turned twenty-one.

I am truly pathetic, he thought. I'm doing my own laundry and reading *Reader's Digest*. And Tim is probably at a premiere or some party. Life had been so much better when Tim was on the losing end of their sibling power struggle. Perry handled success with much more aplomb than he did laundry.

He looked around the Laundromat. Somewhere, perhaps on MTV, he had gleaned that a coin-op was a great place to meet women. He'd feign ignorance over some tough laundry problem and an attractive single woman would take pity on him, explaining the difference between fine hand washables and bath towels. Then he'd take her next door to the Coffee Bean to thank her. Love would blossom. She'd love him so much, she'd never, no matter how much money was at stake, fire him from his own show. And she'd never cozy up to a prima donna like Heather Windward. The people who do their own laundry are real people, he thought.

Real *old* people, he realized as he looked around. Senior citizens do their own laundry, judging from this crowd. This might be a great place to find a surrogate grandmother, but it was no place to find a girlfriend.

At least Tim was alone. Perry took some comfort in that. No one ever seemed to truly *like* Tim, and Tim was unable to bond. While it was true that Perry had made a few errors in judgment when it came to the women he bonded with, at least he was capable of a relationship. That's more than Tim could say.

It was sometime during the rinse cycle that guilt set in. While Perry was quite sure that at that particular moment, he didn't much like his brother, he was willing to accept the possibility that his own sad situation had warped his thinking. When your mother's a pseudo-shrink, you do learn to be a bit analytical, and Perry—sitting in a hot, stuffy Laundromat that reeked of lint and chlorine bleach—was miserable. It wasn't Tim's fault. But it certainly wasn't Perry's fault, either.

The further he spiraled into self-pity, the more convinced Perry became that he simply wasn't meant to do his own laundry. At the very least, he could have his shirts done—how expensive could that be? And really, wasn't fluff-and-fold an amazing bargain? Shoving quarters into these machines adds up, he thought, and miniature boxes of Tide do not come at miniature prices. Plus, I'd have to buy an iron—God knows how much a good iron costs.

By the time his clothes were done drying, Perry had made two important decisions. This was his last trip to a Laundromat—ever! Tonight, he'd go over his budget very carefully. Perhaps if he trimmed a little here and tightened his belt a little there, he could once again start dropping his clothes off at Flair Cleaners. Hell, he could probably hire back the cleaning lady he'd laid off last week. It might be pricey, but given the depths of the depression he felt coming on, it would be much cheaper than therapy.

## Just Like Real Life

**"I can't tell you** how much I appreciate this," said Simon, answering the front door of his Coldwater Canyon house.

Sandy had been surprised to get the early-morning phone call from Simon, who had never once called her at home before. On the phone, he was awkward and cryptic, mumbling something about the Lincoln being disabled and the tow truck driver taking all his cash and how he needed a ride to work. It wasn't the kind of call you usually got from your boss.

"It was quite a night last night, let me tell you," said Simon as he ushered Sandy into the house. "First, the Lincoln died—simply died. Not even the power locks would work, let alone the engine. Of course, I'm not a member of the Auto Club. I used to be, but I wasn't paying attention and it just lapsed—it's been so long since I've had a car break down. So I called a tow truck, but he would take only cash. Well, he gouged me for eighty dollars just to tow the car to the dealer, and that left me merely enough money to take a cab home. Have you ever taken a cab in this city? It's thirty dollars to get anywhere, apparently. No wonder no one takes cabs. That took every bit of cash I had—none of these thieves takes credit cards, which is insane. When I awoke this morning, I realized I was a prisoner in my own home. No car. No cash for a cab. I racked my brains to figure out whom I could call. Frankly, my first instinct was to call Tim, but let's face it—given his hours, I'd just wake him up, and that would be uncomfortable for all concerned. And then I remembered that you lived nearby. I hope you don't mind."

"It's no problem at all," said Sandy. "Being without a car is the worst."

"I must feed the dog. You understand. Feel free to look around." Simon headed toward the kitchen, and then Sandy heard the whir of an electric can opener and the happy jumps of Simon's golden retriever.

The entry and living room to the right were tastefully decorated, even if it all seemed a bit impersonal. It wasn't a house that shouted out, I'm Simon, whatever that might mean. Sandy poked her head through the door on the left, where you'd assume a den or family room might be. There was a large room, totally barren—not a stick of furniture or even a box. She wandered down the hall. Two more rooms—bedrooms?—were equally barren, as if no one lived here at all. At the end of the hall was the master bedroom. Thankfully, like the living room, it had furniture. Nice furniture, like one of those fake rooms you'd find in the furniture section of a department store.

"Have you lived here long?" she asked when Simon returned.

"Oh, yes," said Simon. "My wife found this house when we first moved out here. I didn't much like it at the time, but she was so reluctant to move to L.A., I assumed it was a compromise worth making. It didn't work out. She stayed less than a year—a very unhappy year for both of us, between losing my magazine and her hatred of L.A.—just long enough to decorate the living room and our bedroom. Then she went back to New York. We were going to have a commuter marriage, until we figured things out. Commuter marriages don't work, by the way. I've never heard of one that has. But it was an amicable divorce, I'm happy to say. She's remarried to an editor at the *New York Times* and we have very civilized dinners, the three of us, when I'm back east."

"And you were never inclined to buy a futon or a ficus or something, just to give those other rooms a lived-in look?"

"I've been meaning to," said Simon somewhat mournfully. "But work seems to get in the way."

"How about a smaller house? Maybe a condo?"

"I'm used to this," said Simon. "And then there's the dog to think about. He's happy here, and I'd like to think that I'm capable of making at least one living thing happy in my personal life." He let loose with a nervous laugh. "If only dogs could drive, I could have saved you this extra effort."

"Just think of the decorating ideas I've picked up," joked Sandy. "You're going to save me a fortune if I ever get a house."

Tim dragged himself to work late, as usual. It seemed even later to Sandy, who was dying to tell him about her visit to Simon's. Her head popped over the cubicle wall even before Tim managed to sit down. She rapidly downloaded everything she had seen.

"Totally empty rooms?" asked Tim quizzically.

"More than one," Sandy assured him. "And he's lived there for years."

"Do you know what it sounds like?" said Tim. "It sounds like a movie set. Are you sure it had a ceiling and four real walls? Were there spotlights overhead?"

"No, it was just like a real house. Except for furniture."

"Sort of sad, isn't it?" said Tim, standing and looking toward Simon's office. "You'd think by this time in his life, he'd have a real life."

"He almost does," said Sandy. "It was just like real life, only a bit less."

"No wife, no kids, no furniture, no one to take him to work when his car breaks down? That's more than 'a bit less.' "

"He had *me*," pointed out Sandy. "And even you can't do much better than that."

# Asthma Awareness: A Personal Commitment

**Sandy searched her memory,** from earliest child-hood to present day, contemplating virtually every year of her life, and came up with one inescapable conclusion: This was the worst cold she'd ever had.

"This is no ordinary cold," she told Tim, her head resting on her desk.

Tim stood in her cubicle doorway and pondered the mess before him.

"Are you running a fever? Any unusual symptoms?" he asked.

"I'm too weak to take my temperature. I've never been this sick in my life."

"You said that last month, remember? You were sick when we went shopping."

"This is different. I've been sick too long for this to be a cold. It's something worse, I just know it."

"What do you mean, you've been sick too long? You were well yesterday."

"You don't understand."

"Why don't you go home? We can cancel tomorrow night. That will give you the whole weekend to get better."

"We can't cancel tomorrow night. I bought food. It'll go bad."

"But you're too sick to cook it."

"It's already cooked. All it needs is reheating. Even you could do it."

Great, thought Tim. Just what I need. Out of kindness to a friend, I cancel a date with the best-looking man in Los Angeles, agree to sit in her dainty miniature Martha Stewart apartment to watch the Miss America Pageant, twist my brother's arm to join us, and now she tells me I have to serve dinner, too? Of course, Sandy would have done it for him, and that left him little choice.

It actually wasn't that hard, when it came right down to it. Most of the take-out food was microwavable, and since Sandy's taste buds were out of commission, he only had to worry about Perry's complaints.

"Someone's at the door," Sandy moaned, resting Camille-like on her sofa, kept warm by a brown afghan and hugging a box of Kleenex Cold Care. "It's probably your brother."

"This is a very nice apartment," said Perry, looking around and taking off his jacket.

"It's been in a book," said Tim, responding on Sandy's behalf. "One of those interior design books you can buy at the car wash."

"The car wash on Sepulveda?" asked Perry. "I thought they only sold those weird self-actualization books. And Junior Mints and Velcro visor organizers."

"Sepulveda West Car Wash has its finger on the public's pulse. We want to be happy, and we can be happier in pretty surroundings. It's the inner and outer approach to contentment."

"Hello?" said Sandy feebly, tired of being ignored. "Hellooooo? Sick girl here. Attention must be paid."

"You're looking very . . . terminal tonight," offered Perry.

"I feel terminal. But if I have to die, I want to die watching Miss America. Then you can both tell the press I died doing what I loved best."

There are few things in life more frightening than a beauty pageant. The trio sat riveted to the bizarre sight of eighteen-year-olds who looked like they were forty-four, of truly ugly women in a contest about beauty, of hair and teeth and smiles that were so unnatural, household pets would growl at the TV.

"Miss Kentucky is an advocate for sexual abstinence," announced Donny Osmond.

"I was just like Miss Kentucky for two years," offered Tim, "except for me, it was unintentional and I tried to keep it quiet."

"Miss Indiana's personal commitment is to asthma awareness," said Donny.

"Does anyone here have asthma?" asked Tim.

"Not that I'm aware of," answered Perry on cue. They laughed hysterically.

"I don't want you two to think that I'm not laughing because I'm sick," said Sandy. "I'm not laughing because you're not funny."

That made them laugh even more.

As the judges readied to narrow the field to ten semifinalists, Tim stretched. "Is there any way I could check my E-mail?" he asked.

"I have AOL on the computer in my bedroom," said Sandy.

Tim headed for the bedroom and Perry again raved about

the apartment. "I'm not surprised it was in a book; you have a real eye."

"Thank you," said Sandy. "And remember, I'm responsible for Tim's new look, and we've seen how well that worked."

"I know. Young Timothy has landed a semifamous actor boyfriend. I didn't think I'd ever see something like that. You must have a real talent when it comes to makeovers."

"That's mean," said an indignant Sandy. "Tim's a wonderful person."

"I know, I know," said Perry, backpedaling. "He *is* totally wonderful. It's just that we won't see him in a Calvin Klein ad anytime soon."

"That's ironic, coming from his identical twin."

"Who would know better? Anyway, he's got a boyfriend who could be a Calvin Klein model—that's the next best thing," said Perry.

"Have you seen those pictures of him?" Sandy sighed. "He must spend six hours a day at the gym."

"It's just genes," said Perry. "It's always genes."

"Great genes," agreed Sandy. "At least on the outside. But bad brain genes. It's not like he has it all."

There was an awkward pause. Perry leaned forward to break the silence. "I know you think I'm a jerk," he said softly.

"I can't believe Tim told you I said that," said Sandy indignantly. "I'll kill him."

Perry laughed. "So it's true. Tim never said a word, but I could tell."

Sandy suddenly felt her temperature spike well into the triple digits, but before she could dig herself out of the hole she was in, Tim returned.

"Who wants to bet on the semifinalists?" he asked.

"Miss Hawaii, definitely," said Sandy. "And New York and California always make it. Texas, too."

"I'll say Arizona, Maryland, Texas, Florida, Maine, Illinois, Wyoming, New Mexico, Indiana, and Pennsylvania," insisted Tim.

"You are so crazy," countered Sandy. "They're all dogs. You're out of your mind."

"I think Tim is pretty close," agreed Perry. "I say he gets eight of ten at least—maybe more."

"You're crazy, too. I may have a fever, but you two are delirious."

"Texas will win," said Tim smugly.

"Oh, absolutely," said Perry. "No doubt. None at all."

"She weighs a hundred and eighty pounds if she weighs an ounce," yelled Sandy, exhausting herself. "You two know nothing about beauty pageants."

"We'll see," said Tim.

When all ten of Tim's predictions made the semifinals, Sandy began to feel taken advantage of. When Miss Texas walked down the runway, tears streaming, crown askew, she knew she had been had.

"How did you do that?" she asked.

"He checked it on AOL," said Perry. "The pageant was live in the East, but on tape for us. He ruins the Emmys, too. You know Tim—he has to know everything first."

"I hate you both," said Sandy firmly. "I really hate you."

Perry and Tim made a stab at cleaning up. It wasn't the greatest job, but it was well intentioned. Then they said good night and left together.

Outside, under a streetlight, Perry took a small squeeze bottle of Purelle hand sanitizer from his jacket.

"Want some?" he asked, quickly disinfecting his hands.

"You bet," said Tim. "I was going crazy in there."

Perry took out a small jar and unscrewed the lid. "How about some C?"

"How powerful are they?" asked Tim.

"A thousand."

"Give me three," Tim said, hand outstretched.

"You want echinacea, too?" offered Perry, pulling out another jar.

"Vitamin C *and* echinacea?" marveled Tim. "What are you, a GNC franchise?"

"I can't afford to miss work," said Perry. "I've been taking them all day to ward off Sandy's germs."

"I'm very impressed," said Tim. "But I'd be more impressed if you'd also brought zinc."

Perry laughed. "It's in the car. Honest."

"Sometimes, you're just the best brother in the world," said Tim. "The absolute best."

## Perry Lands at an "A" Table

**Perry looked at it** this way. His old life hadn't worked out very well, so it was time to make some changes. Show business had disappointed him. Nancy had betrayed him. The biggest switch—the job shift—was under way with the new job at Crosswinds, aka "the antistudio." Now it was time for a social adjustment. He needed the anti-Nancy.

Sandy looked at it this way. She was in her rebuilding year. While Perry's life had suddenly and unexpectedly combusted like the Federal Building in Oklahoma City, Sandy's life had drifted leisurely out of its proper place, as if she had fallen asleep while floating on an inner tube, only to awaken so far from shore that it frightened her. She needed someone with her same desire in order to stay tethered and not wander into danger.

So when Perry called Sandy and asked if she wanted to be his date at the annual Crosswinds fund-raiser, it seemed like the most natural of developments. Except for the Tim problem, of course. She wasn't exactly cheating on Tim; that would have been impossible, given the reality of the situation. And it wasn't as if Perry was doing anything wrong, either. One of the great things about having a gay brother is that you're never chasing the same girls.

And yet they both immediately agreed it was best not to tell Tim, at least not yet.

It was probably best not to tell Tim about the fund-raiser at all. It was too perfect a story for Tim's sarcastic take on Hollywood. The location was the Bel-Air Bay Club, a stately megamansion overlooking the ocean, with an elegant ballroom, and massive catering facilities. Crosswinds was only too happy to rent it out for its once-a-year attempt to bleed the parents for an additional several hundred thousand dollars.

It takes money to make money. And Crosswinds knew how to make money. The decorations turned the club into an exact replica of Prince Rainier's palace in Monaco, only nicer. The theme, Midnight in Monaco, was carried out to the most minute detail. An orchestra played for dancers. Wolfgang Puck himself manned the kitchen, and he didn't even have children at the school.

Those who did have kids at Crosswinds were even more famous. "I feel like I'm at Lew Wasserman's funeral," said Sandy as they wandered from the beach to the ballroom and back again. "I've never seen so many stars and studio heads in my life."

Stellar parents were everywhere. Ray Romano was listed as emcee. Tom Petty would be doing a musical number. Ed Ruscha had designed the centerpieces. Jeffrey Katzenberg had volunteered to be auctioneer.

Perry was even more dumbstruck. Only a short time ago, he'd been on track to become one of these people. Now he baby-sat their kids.

"Perry, welcome to Midnight in Monaco." It was Bob Parrish, the unctuous headmaster. "And who do we have here?"

"Bob, this is Sandy Moore. Sandy, Bob Parrish is the founder and headmaster at Crosswinds."

"Sandy, I'm going to steal Perry away for just a few minutes. I promise I'll have him back before you know he's gone."

When they had gained a safe distance from Sandy, Bob's tone became rude and challenging. "I don't understand. What is *she* doing here?"

"What's the matter? She's my date. What's the problem?" Perry was baffled.

"You're a teacher, Mr. Newman. Teachers don't bring dates to the school events. You're lucky we allow teachers to come here at all. This evening exists for a very specific purpose—to raise money. Every seat at every table is valuable. Every seat represents thousands of dollars of potential donations for Crosswinds. Unless your little friend has a very large checkbook, I suggest you call her a cab right now."

Sandy was out of earshot, but Rubin Carson wasn't. Rubin was probably the most powerful parent at the school, and maybe even the richest, which, given the crowd, was a significant distinction. He was president of the school's board of trustees; the new gym would bear his name (and his wife's, of course). It had taken only one phone call from Rubin to secure the Bel-Air Bay Club, and only two phone calls to get Ray Romano to serve as emcee. He'd also personally donated first-class airfare to London for the evening's auction, and threw in a stay at his London apartment as part of the deal.

He was an older man, more likely to be a grandfather to a

Crosswinds student than a father, but the first part of his life has been spent creating a series of monumentally successful TV shows—at one time, Rubin Carson's creations held four of the top ten Nielsen slots for an entire year. After his twelfth hit show, he began directing movies. With their more leisurely pace, films allowed him time to marry a younger woman and have children. He doted on his children with the same single-mindedness he had used to amass his fortune.

"Bob, why don't you introduce me? If I'm not mistaken, this must be our new English teacher."

Bob uncomfortably handled the introductions.

"I'm pleased to meet you, Mr. Carson," said Perry. "I'm a big admirer of your work."

"And I'm pleased to meet you, especially since my son Alex is in your class," said Rubin with a mischievous glint. "Bob, I was hoping Perry and his lady friend could join me at my table. Could you arrange that for me?"

"Of course," stammered Bob. "I'll take care of that right now." And he was gone.

"Thank you," said Perry. "I'm new, and I'm afraid I violated some protocol that I knew nothing about."

"Think nothing of it," said Rubin. "And don't worry about Bob. He doesn't hold grudges. I don't allow him to."

Perry returned to Sandy, who, despite her best intentions, had been a total wallflower in his absence. But she hadn't been bored. She had seen too much power schmoozing of the most unlikely sort.

"I found our table," he said. "I think you'll be impressed."

She smiled and thought about Tim and how much he would have enjoyed watching what she'd just seen—Anthony Edwards, Susan Sarandon, Mick Foley, Shannon Tweed, and Milos Forman huddled in a corner, drinking white wine and wildly enjoying a private joke. Why not? They were all in the same business.

# Why Martha Stewart Is
# Really Betty Friedan in Drag

**Ann's party, which had** seemed like such a fun project only a couple of weeks ago, now loomed as a dark and ugly obligation. For the first time since the boys had left home, Ann realized how alone she was. Back then, she'd had live-in help, a series of illegal aliens who lived in the small utility room off the kitchen and did the unpleasant work that women in both upper and lower Los Angeles rarely did. But they were gone now—all of those wonderful women who didn't mind scrubbing floors, washing windows, and scouring bathtubs. On the plus side, it allowed Ann and Syd to move the washer and dryer in from the garage and place it in the more convenient utility room. But there was a price to pay: It meant that Ann was flying solo, trying to maintain the house despite her numerous commitments.

Ann was old enough to remember housework. She was old enough to recall her mother keeping a spotless home—and that was before Dustbusters or paper towels. She remembered reading countless household tips in women's magazines, about soaking diamond rings in baking soda, squeezing fresh lemon into the wash, and removing bloodstains with club soda. But then there was Betty Friedan and *The Feminine Mystique.* That was good, mostly—Ann owed her many careers to Betty's inspiration—but there was a downside. Suddenly, cleaning house was demonized, a symbol of oppression, like picking cotton or shining shoes. It was beneath everyone—man, woman, or child—and even the women's magazines banished household tips in favor of advice on orgasm maintenance and twenty ways to drive your man wild in bed.

Beneath anyone who spoke English, that is. Maintaining the Newman household was never beneath Consuelo, Maria, Nicole, or Sarita. Ann was quietly grateful for that faulty fence that separated the United States and Mexico and for the fact that *The Feminine Mystique* had never been translated into Spanish.

It wasn't that Ann was indifferent to how her house looked. Quite the contrary. She read Martha Stewart religiously. Martha understood. She also wanted to liberate women from drudgery, and took the fun part of housework and elevated it to an art form, a chance for someone like Ann, who had never really felt comfortable giving full vent to her creative side, a chance to express herself. Or at least *think* about expressing herself. Even better, it alleviated the guilt Ann felt about subcontracting the real work to Maria or Consuelo and concentrating on something that satisfied her need for self-expression—like centerpieces. That's what made Martha rich—repackaging the best part of housework in a bright new bow and making it hip. Those Martha Stewart projects were daunting, but at least they weren't demeaning. Betty Friedan would be proud.

Ann paced the living room floor as she waited for the party planner. Her head was swimming with cuisines from around the world. Cajun? Mexican? Italian? Some sort of barbecue arrangement? And music. And decorations. She didn't want this to be too stuffy, but it had to be nice. She tried to keep a particularly horrible image out of her mind: the time Syd had dragged her to a party at the home of the dealership's longtime mechanic. Not only was it in a questionable part of the Valley (and it was easy for Ann to forget that those areas existed on her side of hill); it featured a twelve-foot subway sandwich as the main attraction. Ann had never seen anything quite like it before, and she was sure she never wanted to again.

"You have the perfect backyard for a party," said Rhett, the party planner Linda had enthusiastically recommended, based on something she'd overheard while waiting for a parent-teacher conference. "Close your eyes for a minute and picture this. Small white lights in all the trees and bushes. We cover the pool—I know that sounds big, but it's very inexpensive—and put up a buffet table with the best Mexican food from El Cholo and a bar serving fresh margaritas and Corona beer. On the lawn, we'll have fifteen tables with brightly colored tablecloths. Over by the hill, a three-piece mariachi band—don't worry, they won't stroll and they won't be loud. Or, if you want, we could stick a disc jockey over there—live music might be overkill."

He turned slowly, examining the yard for more inspiration, something that would take this event to a new level. He closed his eyes and rubbed his temples. Finally, his muse struck.

"Now imagine this," he said emotionally. "All the walkways and all the tables festooned with hand-painted luminarias with real candles. Can you see it?"

Ann could not only see it; it nearly moved her to tears. She had been so concerned, and yet the answer was now so clear. She was proud of herself for having turned to Linda. That had been the key moment in this party being a big success, and Ann had done it without any help at all. Her instincts had told her to call Linda, and once again, her instincts had been right.

Even Syd agreed the price was reasonable, and Ann looked forward to letting that sense of calm wash over her once the party planner had left. The tension, the worry—it had been debilitating. She had suffered a constant headache, and worse yet, she knew that something was bothering Syd and she hadn't been there for him. If nothing else, they had always stood by each other, and she felt guilty for letting her stupid party distract her.

Rhett left, and Ann sat in her favorite chair and waited. She tapped her foot. She skimmed absentmindedly through a copy of *Vanity Fair*. But she wasn't relaxed. There was no sense of relief surging through her body. Her party would be perfect, and yet it wasn't having the desired effect. As a licensed marriage and family counselor, Ann knew the warning signs. She took her pulse. It was a tad fast, but nothing to be concerned about—or maybe it was.

Something deeper was going on in Ann's psyche. She had enough self-awareness to know that she was an extremely complicated woman, and this unfortunate sense of anxiety might require more extreme measures. She took her pulse again. It was still elevated. How much more proof did she need?

She went upstairs to her room and got out her phone book. It was time to call Dr. Judy Berkowitz, perhaps the finest psychologist in all of Studio City, the author of *Keeping Your Eye on I*, a self-published book on assertiveness, host of a public-access show on cable, and the only woman Ann knew personally who had ever been in *People* magazine. It had been three years since their last session, and it was clear to Ann that it was time for a tune-up.

## Tim Slips into Something European

**Antonio was standing curbside** as Tim pulled up, a gesture that Antonio probably didn't give a second's thought to but which was fraught with meaning for Tim. *My TV star boyfriend is so eager to see me, he waits outside the restaurant.* The fact that Antonio was one of the best-looking guys in Boy's Town—that stretch of Santa Monica Boulevard in West Hollywood famous for great-looking gay men—made it mean even more.

Of course, there was a challenge ahead. Tim was now forced to parallel park on a busy street in front of his boyfriend. That's pressure. He remembered when Ann was studying to be a boil-in-the-pouch shrink and came home exhausted one night. "You won't believe the day I had," she'd said, slumping into a chair. "I had to make a left-hand turn in front of my psychology professor." Ann would understand what Tim was going though. Luckily, Honda Civics are small, easy to maneuver, and besides, Tim had been driving Hondas even before he was of age, when his dad would let the two boys drive around the unpopulated sections of Newman's Super Honda late at night, after closing, making their friends very jealous.

Tim slipped into the parking space like a real grown-up. He almost waited for Antonio to blurt out, Hey, great parking job. Instead, Antonio shrugged. "I really don't understand why you're still driving that thing," he said. "You're on the verge of being a famous writer. You should have something special."

"I'll be getting rid of it soon," said Tim. "My dad can get me an Acura Integra at cost."

"Whatever." Antonio snorted with disdain.

"What do you mean, 'whatever'?"

"I'd just rather see you in something European, that's all. It's more you."

"I'd rather see me in something European, too. But European costs money."

"Not that much."

"Is there some sort of bargain Mercedes I don't know about?" asked Tim.

"Screw Mercedes. That's a car for old people. You need a BMW. Not a big one—those are for old people, too. Just a small one. A three-series. They're cheap, but really cool."

Tim had to agree that there was something very cool about a BMW, and he actually liked those smaller three-series Beemers much better than the big pseudo-limos. BMWs, as Simon James would say, were very upper Los Angeles. A Honda Civic couldn't be more lower L.A. With the extra syndication money and the likely IPO jackpot in his future, a modest BMW didn't seem like such an extravagance. He liked the idea of telling the valet at Asia de Cuba—any valet, really—"It's the white BMW, please."

"Maybe I will," mused Tim.

"Why wait?" snapped Antonio. "Let's do it now."

As they headed toward Beverly Hills BMW just a few miles away, Tim couldn't help but think that he had just wasted a spectacular job of parallel parking.

Normally, a tousled-haired twenty-six-year-old journalist in jeans and a T-shirt would have as much luck getting noticed by a BMW salesman as he would by the president of Paramount. But with Antonio leading the way, the finely tuned antenna of even the densest car salesman picked up the signal.

There are two lessons to be learned in visiting a BMW dealership: There's no such thing as a cheap BMW, and the salespeople and surroundings adopt a certain affectation befitting the product. Customers sat in leather chairs far posher than the uncomfortable metal chairs his dad used to decorate Newman's Super Honda. The salespeople wore elegant suits and had offices, not cubicles, with carpet and music and Starbucks coffee.

Tim started at the top of the three-series, then moved downward, each model being slightly more basic than the one before. Four doors became two. CD players became tape decks. Leather became cloth. Automatics became stick shifts. And although the price dropped each time, it was still a staggering amount.

At the very bottom of the BMW food chain was the 318ti, a car that Tim knew would have been humble even by Kia standards. A tiny hatchback, it was clearly smaller than his Civic, but it claimed to seat four, even if the backseat was barely suitable for a double amputee. It looked more like a Pez dispenser than a car, but it had a sunroof, and it said BMW on the hood, on the trunk, and on each of the four tiny little wheels. With tax and license and despite hard bargaining (which sounded like begging), it was under thirty thousand dollars—at least by a few bucks. With eight thousand for trading in the Civic, it was practically affordable. Before he knew it, Tim was drowning in paperwork, staggered by tax and license, and listening to a spirited sales pitch for LoJack.

"What have I done?" asked Tim when Antonio took him out for a celebratory dinner.

"You did the right thing," Antonio assured him. "You look great in that car, really sexy. And BMWs hold their value. You can upgrade in no time."

"I've never bought a car without my father before," moaned Tim. "None of us has. He owns a dealership, for Christ's sake. He won't understand."

"He knows what cars mean in L.A.," said Antonio. "Who would better understand the importance of owning a BMW in our business than a man who sells cars for a living? He can't have any delusions about Honda, can he?"

"Why don't you come with me when I show it to him and find out?"

"Taking me home to meet the parents? Isn't that a bit bold for the good son who's still in the closet?"

"I'm serious. They're having a party and I have to go. They'll expect me to bring a friend, so that won't seem weird. And my dad will be much too busy to spend time berating me for a foolish purchase."

Antonio was stunned at the prospect. "A party in the Valley with old people." He smiled. "How can I say no?"

"We won't have to stay long," said Tim. "And you'll get to see my roots, get a sense of where I come from."

"I guess," said Antonio, sounding only slightly convinced. "Maybe that means you'll write another story about me. I've got new projects coming up, and you're going to need stuff to write about."

Tim didn't hear him. His BMW key came with a built-in light to help you find the keyhole. Tim flashed it on and off rhythmically. So far, it was the only part of the purchase that pleased him.

That night in his apartment, Tim started throwing up. He didn't know why, but he narrowed the culprit down to three possibilities. One: bad shrimp. Two: the inevitability of hearing his father saying, "I could have gotten you a new Honda with leather seats and a six-disc changer for less than half what that . . . that thing just cost you. What were you thinking?" Three: He was taking Antonio to his home, where he'd meet Tim's parents, his brother, and assorted relatives and family friends.

Any one of those could cause nausea. It was amazing that the combined forces of all three didn't kill him right there on the bathroom floor.

# Syd and the King

**Well past midnight but** before dawn on those nights when misery made sleep impossible, Syd Newman would discreetly crawl out of bed and move downstairs into the den. There, guided only by the light of his TV, he'd fumble for his favorite group of videos, then picking one at random, plug it into the VCR. If it was chilly out—or if it was so warm that the air conditioning was working overtime—he'd also pull out a small electric heater and turn it on. The blue glow of the TV and the warm hum of the space heater were soothing, part of the ritual that helped Syd combat insomnia.

He was a little embarrassed by his tape collection. He didn't care enough about TV to have many videos. He didn't have a fan's mentality. He left that to Ann, who fell in and out of infatuation with various celebrities and fads while stolid Syd got up, went to work, came home, and good-naturedly supported Ann on her enthusiasm of the moment.

"You're impossible to shop for," Ann often complained. "You have no interests, so no one can buy you anything." But that seemed like a lousy reason to find a hobby, so Syd remained Syd-like, a rock of reliability in a flaky, neurotic world.

Unless you counted his small collection of Johnny Carson videos. Tim had given them to him for Father's Day, and if he had known how often his father watched them, he'd have known he'd scored a gift home run against impossible odds. It was just a lucky guess on Tim's part, however. He wasn't too young to remember when Johnny Carson was king, but he was much too young to realize what Carson's reign was like.

For his entire adult life, Syd had watched *The Tonight Show*. Not religiously, not even regularly. It was there, after the news, if he was so inclined. Over the years, he dipped in and out of Johnny watching, never loyal enough to be a fan but appreciative that Carson demonstrated reliability—that one value that seemed missing everywhere else.

There were periods, however, when Syd was indeed a stalwart viewer. During periods of emotional upheaval, during illness or depression, or around the time his own father died, he found himself drawn to the TV every night at 11:30 by some irresistible force. Long before there was Prozac, Syd had Johnny Carson. The world around him might be shattering into pieces, but Johnny Carson was always Johnny Carson. It didn't hurt that Johnny's midwestern stoicism reminded Syd in many ways of his dad, or at least of the way Syd wanted to be perceived by those around him.

He settled back to watch the *Best of Carson, Volume 2: The Master of Laughs.* Syd's own life at that very moment was frayed and unraveling. There was the ugly struggle for control of Newman's Super Honda. There was Ann's party, which could hardly come at a worse time. There were the boys, who reminded him of the guy on the old *Ed Sullivan Show* who used to spin dinner plates on long sticks—no sooner would he steady one plate than another would start to wobble. Perry and Tim were like that. As soon as one seemed to get a solid footing, the other started sliding down the hill. He worried about Tim most of all. Perry, despite the questionable taste in women he'd shown thus far, would eventually get married and have a family. There would be Sunday dinners to anchor him for the rest of his life. But Tim! If Ann and the kids and Johnny Carson had kept Syd sane, what was in store for Tim? What happens to people who don't have regular Sunday dinners with family? he wondered. That sometimes seemed like the glue that held it all together.

If Johnny Carson and Sunday dinners kept Syd from becoming unstuck in life, then it was Syd who served that same purpose for Ann. Ann was on a longer leash, and she could easily wander off into trouble or some sort of unhappiness. Syd was on a much shorter leash, and he kept his eye on Ann, reeling her in when she was lost or drifted perilously close to the ledge.

It was Ann, he knew, who kept the boys in check. There was something about mothers and sons. No matter what, they wanted to please her. It was Pavlovian. They came to Sunday dinner not to please Syd, but to please Ann. When Ann was out of town and the boys kept tabs on him, it was to make Ann happy. Ann wanted them to do that, and she was thrilled when they came through. Even now, her approval made them beam, even involuntarily.

The heat from the small electric heater blew at Syd's bare feet while overhead he could feel the chill of the air conditioner. I've become Richard Nixon, he thought. Nixon used to crank up the air conditioning in the White House and then light a roaring fire in the fireplace. Syd understood. It was like driving in a convertible in February with the heat up full blast and the top down.

He remembered Carson's last hurrah. Only a few weeks before the last *Tonight Show* with Johnny Carson, the L.A. riots had broken out. Although the Newmans were a safe distance over the hill from any trouble, it had been unsettling. Even more unsettling was the fact that the local riot coverage pre-empted *The Tonight Show* for two nights, two of the last nights Carson would even appear on TV. Depressed by the events around him, Syd hadn't even had the solace of Johnny Carson. As he watched parts of Los Angeles burn, he couldn't help but wonder what was on those two shows. Apparently, the local NBC affiliate knew that there were many Syds out there, and it ran the unaired shows a few days later, over the weekend. All was not lost.

As he watched the tape of a very young Garry Shandling chatting with Johnny, Syd realized what was keeping him awake. His dealership was slipping away, and he lacked the financial clout to keep it from happening. He couldn't afford to buy out his partners, and while he and Ann wouldn't starve if he lost the battle, that seemed beside the point. He couldn't imagine life without Newman's Super Honda. It was like a Sunday dinner—it was so much a part of his identity that without it, he wasn't sure he'd have a reason to go on living. Not that he'd kill himself, exactly, but he'd lose the will to live, his resistance would drop, and he'd develop cancer or his heart would not have enough reason to expend the extra effort to keep him alive. He had to save the dealership, because if the dealership went, he'd go, too. And who'd look after Ann so that she could mind the boys? Who'd pay for the Sunday dinners?

## Ordering Off the Menu

**"Do you ever miss New York?"** Tim asked Simon, just to make conversation as they awaited their food at lunch. Sandy was being unusually quiet, and Simon had been showing the stress of too many intense high-level budgetary meetings. Tim was hyper and happy, excited by his big purchase and new romance.

"I did at first," said Simon. "But the longer you're away, the more New York comes into focus. It's a city fueled by the biggest inferiority complex you can imagine. Especially publishing. Everyone is obsessed with his or her place in the universe; it's a high school pecking order. You think that people in show business are into status? Here, status comes easily. You do well, you make money, and you buy a Lexus. Everyone sees your Lexus, so they know you're doing well. Your point is made and you can move on with the rest of your life. But not in New York. Not in the publishing world. God no. Everyone lives in the same area, and everyone makes the same amount of money, so you have to express your status by a constant pitiful attack on everyone around you. It's who you know. It's what party you were invited to. It's who you sit next to at dinner. It's the location of your table at the Four Seasons. God knows, it's the fact that you can order something off the fucking menu at the Four Seasons. Have you ever seen anyone order something off the menu in L.A.?"

"I've never even heard of ordering off the menu," said Tim. "Although I can imagine what it is."

"And you eat with the most status-consumed assholes in this city. Do you know why they don't order off the menu? I'll tell you. They don't have to. They don't have to define themselves by the fact that 'chef' will make them something special. They're already special, because the valet has put their Lexus in a prime position out front, so they can relax. Or it's just so well known that they're rich and successful, they needn't remind you. That's why Michael Eisner can wear jeans to the Grill. He doesn't have to advertise his success by wearing Prada. But you do in New York. In New York, you can never relax."

"But those guys have a big New Year's Eve bash, and we've got nothing," offered Sandy.

"That's another thing that drives me crazy!" Simon was so worked up now that Tim feared he might have a stroke. "New Yorkers brag about their big New Year's Eve bash in Times Square! In Egypt, they'll put on an event at the pyramids. In Greece, they'll have a big event at the Parthenon. Places with significance. Do you remember the millennium show at the Eiffel Tower? And yet New Yorkers gravitate to the seediest spot in town for New Year's, a place maybe a notch more interesting than Hollywood Boulevard, and if that's not bad enough, they're proud of it. I mean, really, what could be more juvenile and silly than bragging about your New Year's party? It's high school, I tell you. And not even a good high school."

"So," said Sandy. "I guess it's safe to say that you don't miss New York."

"Oh, I miss it," he said ruefully. "I miss it every day. I just hate myself for it."

Back at the office, Sandy was still amazed by Simon's show of emotion. "Wow," she said. "If I were a shrink, I'd say that wasn't about New York at all, but about something else entirely."

"Like what?" asked Tim.

"Like maybe he's the one who's insecure, not the city of New York. Like maybe he's the one with status issues. How much did that Lincoln Town Car cost, anyway?"

"Is this the wrong time to mention that I bought a BMW?" asked Tim sheepishly.

"Come again?"

"Not a big BMW, just a small BMW. Antonio sort of talked me into it."

"Is it here? Is it in the lot? Can I see it?"

"Sure, it's here. We can go take a look. I'll take you for a drive, if you like."

"I never took you for a status geek, Timothy," said Sandy as they walked into the parking lot. Tim marched her directly to his new car. "Where is it?" she asked.

"This is it," he said. Suddenly, the car looked even smaller and less impressive than it had before. Tim tensed in anticipation.

"This?" Sandy seemed genuinely confused.

"It's so . . ." Sandy searched her data bank for the right word. "It's very—"

"Go ahead, there's nothing you can say that I won't hear from my dad."

"It's small, isn't it?" said Sandy. "I guess you could say that that's a good thing. A lot of people like small cars."

"Yes, it's small."

"I mean, this is the entire car—it almost seems to be missing the back half."

"It's a hatchback. It's supposed to look like that."

"It's a lot smaller than your Civic. . . ." Sandy paused, wishing she could think of something a tad more positive to contribute. Finally, inspiration struck. "I'll bet it gets excellent mileage."

"I'm sure it does," said Tim, crestfallen. "And it handles really well, too. Honest."

"Well, it's German," chirped Sandy. "It should."

It was quiet on the walk back to the office. Sandy tried to undo the damage the teeny-tiny BMW had caused.

"You deserved something nice," she said. "It's like Simon said—now you've made your statement and you can get on with your life."

"I'm not sure what statement I've made." Tim sighed.

"That size doesn't matter?" offered Sandy.

"Oh God," moaned Tim. "Do you know what that car cost me?"

"I've got it," said Sandy. "You're rebelling. You're not just saying yes to BMW, you're saying no to Honda. You're breaking away from parental domination. It's probably very healthy."

"I could have said yes to Kia and saved twenty grand."

"But who wants to tell the valet they have a white Kia?" said Sandy helpfully. "They'd laugh at you. Valets have better cars than Kias."

"Well, thanks for trying," said Tim as he slumped in his chair back in his cubicle. "It's only a car. I can always sell it. I hear even the worst BMWs have great resale."

"Well, there are dumber things than buying a BMW," said Sandy. "Look at me, for example. I did something the other night so bizarre that I've been afraid to tell even you."

"Now's a good time to tell me," said Tim. "I'm a broken man. Nothing you could say would seem as strange as what I've done."

"Are you sure?"

"Positive."

"Really sure? Really, really sure?"

"Hit me with all you've got."

"Good," said Sandy as she quickly packed all her belongings to make a quick getaway. "Remember last Saturday when I told you I had a date?"

"I remember, but you said you didn't want to talk about it."

"Yes, that's the one." Sandy clutched her purse and book bag to her chest.

"Go ahead, shoot. I'm bulletproof."

"I went to a Crosswinds fund-raiser with Perry." Sandy smiled a small smile and waved her hand. "Gotta run. You call your brother and we'll talk tomorrow." And then she vanished. She was out the door before she could hear the dull thud of Tim's head hitting his own desk.

# Learning to Share

**Guilt is a wonderful** motivating factor. It takes you places you'd never go on your own. It was guilt, for instance, that brought Perry to deepest, darkest West Hollywood, to the Koo Koo Roo outlet on Santa Monica Boulevard. He knew it was one of Tim's favorite places to guy-watch—this particular Koo Koo Roo was surrounded by gyms and was a favorite postworkout haunt. Perry was meeting Tim for a quick dinner, but when he went into the restaurant, he found himself surrounded by men so buff that they looked freakish. It was like being a white guy in Watts—everyone in Koo Koo Roo eyed him suspiciously, as if he were some sort of dangerous outsider.

Perry didn't know why he felt so guilty. He hadn't done

anything wrong, except not tell Tim that he was taking Sandy out on a date. That wasn't really so wrong. At worst, it was impolite. He had managed to avoid Tim successfully ever since he'd taken Sandy to the fund-raiser, thinking it was better if Tim heard it from Sandy. That thinking, Perry now realized, was misguided. But every day he waited made the situation worse. So he called Tim, suggested dinner, picked the Koo Koo Roo because he thought it was a show of good faith, and besides, as a teacher, it was one of the few places he could afford. He figured it would also be a nice gesture if he paid.

The scene inside Koo Koo Roo was just too intensely homo for Perry, so he wandered back outside to wait for Tim.

How did it end up that Tim was sometimes his best friend and other times the most annoying person in his life? There were times when being with Tim was the most normal feeling in the world, and other times when hanging out with Tim was like being with Jesse Helms or Dennis Rodman, some alien creature with whom Perry had nothing in common.

Then there was the guilt and jealousy. When Perry landed his show, he felt guilty because Tim didn't have one, too. When Tim got his syndicated column, he felt jealous. The only consolation was that Perry assumed Tim had the same feelings, only more so. Tim was more sensitive—everyone in the family knew that—and it wasn't because he was gay. Oh hell, maybe it was. Perry was never sure. He could look at Tim and see so much of himself, and yet the differences were staggering. Tim had sex with men. Perry usually dealt with it by trying not to think about it and certainly never asking about it. Nor did he talk much about his girlfriends, figuring there'd be too much guilt and jealousy added to the already-overflowing mix. He realized that it kept them from ever being truly close—they could only talk shop and badmouth their parents so much—but maybe that was a good thing. Maybe a little distance between twin brothers helps them find themselves.

Just the idea that Tim would feel normal around this group of vain, creatine-addicted mutants scared Perry. What do I have in common with Tim, anyway? he wondered.

Tim arrived in his white BMW 318ti. Even though Sandy had warned him, Perry was stunned at how small it was. What had Tim been thinking?

"New car," said Perry with a grunt, acknowledging the obvious.

"Don't make fun of it," ordered Tim. "I've suffered enough, and Dad hasn't even seen it yet."

"My lips are sealed," said Perry, eager to make things right.

"What in the hell are we doing here?" asked Tim as they walked inside.

"I thought you liked this place. You said you used to come here for lunch by yourself all the time," answered Perry.

"Well, yeah—but that was when I was bored and unemployed and lonely and I'd come here on hot days and watch a bunch of good-looking guys sit around shirtless and ignore me. That hardly seems to be something you'd be interested in."

"I was trying to make a good impression," said Perry.

"Fuck that. Let's get out of here. I feel fat."

"Me, too," said Perry as they headed up the street for Hugo's, a laid-back pasta place. "I figured I should come begging forgiveness on your turf."

"The Sandy thing?" asked Tim cockily.

"Yes, the Sandy thing. I should have told you. It was rude and weird and passive-aggressive and insensitive and all my other faults."

"It was," agreed Tim. "And I was really mad, and I couldn't figure out why. It wasn't just because you didn't tell me. Even if you had told me beforehand, I would have been mad. I didn't really want to share Sandy, certainly not with you. I've had to share enough with you. I figured that's why you didn't tell me. I wouldn't have told me, either."

"Still, it stunk, and I'm sorry," said Perry. "I don't want to ruin your friendship with Sandy."

"You were smart not to call," said Tim. "I was madder three days ago. I'm better now."

"That's good," said Perry. "I'm relieved."

"And I know we never talk about this stuff. We never have."

"I know. I was just thinking about that."

"You're straight and I'm gay, and there's a certain discomfort there. I still don't really know what went on between you and Nancy, or any girl you've dated. At least with Sandy, I'll have a reliable inside source."

"I don't know why I don't talk about those things. But you never have, either."

"We didn't talk about my love life because I didn't have one. Even now that I do, I can't imagine telling you about it."

"It's not that I don't care," said Perry earnestly.

"I know you care." Tim laughed. "You have to. You're my brother, and Mom would kill you if you didn't care."

"No, I mean I really care. We could start talking about this stuff. It might be good for us."

Tim thought for a moment. "You mean Perry and Tim Newman would sit around, drink a beer, and Perry would talk about his girlfriend of the moment and his feelings and all that sex stuff? And then Tim would talk about the same things, except it would be about a guy?"

There was a long silence.

"Do you want to hear about my night with Antonio? I could tell you. You're a big boy—it won't kill you."

Perry again took too long to answer.

"So, I'm assuming you want to reconsider," Tim said. Perry could be so sincere, it was almost patronizing. They had their relationship terrain staked out, and it hadn't changed much since they were kids. There was no reason to go tinkering with a successful formula.

"You're probably right," admitted Perry. "I guess I don't feel *that* guilty."

# The Disturbed Sciences in Action

**Dr. Judy Berkowitz was** weighing one of the most important questions a psychotherapist can face. It had preyed on her mind all day, distracting her from helping her poor patients, and that wasn't good. Healing was Dr. Judy's passion. But still, important therapeutic decisions cannot be made in haste. She paced her small Sherman Oaks office and asked herself, Is it better to appear on *Politically Incorrect* or *Sally Jessy Raphael*?

Dr. Judy knew that some therapists—those craven publicity hounds constantly hawking their books—would simply appear on both. How sad that is for our profession, thought Dr. Judy. Dr. Judy took her role as a psychotherapist a bit more seriously. Let the others churn out poorly written, barely researched books year after year, using any ghostwriter they could find. Let them whore themselves on talk radio or hokey local TV. No wonder the public had so little faith in psychotherapy. Dr. Judy dared to be different. She spent months interviewing ghostwriters, until she found just the right one—someone with gravitas, like that wonderful woman who had helped Cybill Shepherd with her inspirational tome. It was Dr. Judy who had insisted, even when her agent scoffed, that the book be based on real scientific research, not just clippings from *Redbook*. Sure, it took at little longer and it might not sell as well, but Dr. Judy was confident that her newest book, *Why Women Care and Men Don't*, would help people. And isn't that what it's all about? she thought.

Dr. Judy glanced at her watch. The time she had allotted for self-examination was over. Now it was time to help a patient, one of her favorites, who had returned after a few years' hiatus. Dr. Judy understood. So many of them came back.

Ann Newman was a strong woman, and Dr. Judy felt, modestly, that part of the credit for Ann's incredible strength came from their weekly sessions when her children were still young. Dr. Judy was pleased. The idea of meeting with one of her biggest success stories was a well-timed validation.

For her part, Ann had many questions. Is it possible to get addicted to SAM-e? She was taking four a day, and while she was sure it helped, she didn't want to end up at Betty Ford over some herb. And then their was that gnawing feeling that something wasn't quite right in the Newman family, an uneasiness that kept Ann from concentrating on real issues, like her career.

The office had gone through a remarkable transformation since Ann's last visit. It was brighter and cheerier. The African masks on the wall had been replaced by Navajo wall hangings. The shag carpet was now a glistening darkened wood. The aquarium had been replaced by a tranquil indoor fountain, with water slowly cascading down a sheet of corrugated metal. Ann found the new office much more to her liking.

"Before we even start," said Dr. Judy as they sat opposite each other in two overstuffed chairs from Shabby Chic, "let me just say that you look wonderful. I can tell just by sitting here that you've retained your youthful vigor without eliminating the wisdom one gets from age."

That's so true, thought Ann. Dr. Judy is nothing if not perceptive.

"Let me ask," said Dr. Judy, leaning forward. "How are the girls? Are they doing well in school?"

"Well, they're boys, of course," said Ann. "They're grown and living on the other side of the hill."

"Of course," said Dr. Judy, smiling confidently. "And Paul? Does he still work for NBC."

"It's Syd, actually. He has the Honda dealership in the Valley."

"Good for him," said Dr. Judy. "I think that's a very positive step."

"He's had the dealership for over twenty years," insisted Ann.

"Even better, don't you think?" Dr. Judy beamed. Ann was doing well indeed.

"There are so many things I want to ask you about," said Ann. "I've been taking SAM-e, and I was worried that perhaps I was overdoing it, taking too much."

"I understand." Dr. Judy nodded. "Brain chemistry is so complex that we're just now beginning to understand it. SAM-e, Saint-John's-wort, Celexa, Paxil, Prozac—we live in a wonderful time. We're able to help so many more people than ever before."

"How much SAM-e is too much?" asked Ann.

"Well, that depends, doesn't it?" said Dr. Judy. "Every person is different. What might be too much for you would be just right for Paul."

"That's Syd."

"Of course."

"How would I know?"

"Do you feel as if you're taking too much?" asked Dr. Judy, her brow furrowed and her expression concerned.

"I might," said Ann. "But sometimes I fear I'm not taking enough."

"You know what that tells you, don't you?" said Dr. Judy, relaxing. "That tells you you're taking just the right amount."

"I am so relieved," said Ann.

"That's what I'm here for," said Dr. Judy. "Now let me ask you a question. SAM-e will often provoke vivid and revealing dreams. Do you have any that come to mind?"

Ann paused. She wasn't in the habit of remembering her dreams, and her dreams certainly had seemed no more intense with SAM-e than without it. But there was that dream from this morning. . . .

"I did have a dream. I was in my backyard, and it was terribly overgrown with large thorny plants. In the dream, I'm desperate to get the plants cleared up, because I'm having a party that night. The gardener wasn't my usual gardener, but a hideous dwarf, and his assistant was a very stern and unforgiving blind woman."

"How did you know she was blind?" asked Dr. Judy, interested.

"She wore these large dark glasses. Not sunglasses, but glasses that were solidly dark."

The human mind never ceases to amaze, thought Dr. Judy. This was why her job was never boring.

"This man, he was very ugly, you said?"

"Yes, almost deformed."

"And the woman wore large dark glasses?"

"Yes," said Ann, eager to hear the interpretation.

"Let me try some of my impressions on you," said Dr. Judy. "Maybe they'll be apt. Maybe they won't. Only you will know."

Ann was excited.

"Could this ugly man be a modified, disguised version of someone in your life? Perhaps not someone you know, but someone you've seen, even in a movie or on TV?"

"It's possible," agreed Ann.

"By any chance, did you watch *Politically Incorrect* last night before you went to bed?"

"Why yes! Yes, I did. How did you know?"

"Let me ask you this: Could the hideous dwarf be simply another version of Bill Maher?"

Ann didn't know what to say. There were similarities, and yet she wasn't sure it all made sense.

"And the woman with glasses—is it possible that she's Sally Jessy Raphael?"

"I don't know," said a confused Ann. "Maybe."

"Bear with me here," said Dr. Judy. "Let's just say that I'm right. Let's just say that your dream contains disguised versions of Bill Maher and Sally Jessy Raphael. Why do you think that is?"

"I don't have a clue. I wouldn't know where to begin," protested Ann.

"But you watch both shows, correct?"

"No," said Ann emphatically. "I mean, I'll watch *Politically Incorrect* with Syd sometimes, but I can't imagine watching *Sally Jessy Raphael*."

"That's very interesting," said Dr. Judy. "Do you like *Politically Incorrect*?"

"It's a good show, I guess. They have some interesting guests," answered Ann. "It's funny enough."

"Of course," said Dr. Judy. "Your unconscious is telling you something, and that's important." So important that Dr. Judy immediately wrote it in her notebook: "Yes to PI: no to SJR." She'd call her agent as soon as the session was over to let him know she'd made up her mind.

"Now let's change the subject," she suggested as Ann looked befuddled. "Are you more likely to buy self-help books in a bookstore or on-line?"

# Bong Hits at the Four Seasons

**Why it was at** Perry's apartment and why it happened that night, neither Perry nor Sandy could explain. What started as dinner at the Daily Grill and a movie at the Beverly Connection resulted in Sandy spending the night. It was neither planned nor manipulated, but grew organically out of their third date. Maybe that's why it went so spectacularly well.

It was all too exciting for Perry to fall asleep after. He lay in bed, eyes darting around the room, trying to hold his body perfectly still while he marveled at the turns his life had taken. He was no longer a TV writer, but a schoolteacher. And Sandy was unlike any other girl he had dated. She was a human being and not a career move. Their dinner conversation at the Daily Grill had not been full of invective toward more successful writers, nor a constant stream of half-baked notions followed by the exclamation "Wait a second, that could be a show! What if we put Jon Stewart as the lead and made Ben Stein the wacky night watchman? UPN loves that kind of stuff."

Instead, they talked about normal things—if Tim Newman could be considered normal, for example. He was, for the moment, their common bond, so it was only natural that they'd spend time analyzing him. Tim inspired an odd mixture of awe and concern among his friends and family—awe because he seemed so smart and talented, concern because he so often seemed lost and vulnerable. Perry hadn't spent so much time reliving his childhood since he tried therapy for a few months four years ago. Unlike his shrink, Sandy seemed genuinely interested.

Perry was wide awake as the sun came up, and while Sandy slept soundly—or at least did a better job pretending than Perry was able to—he slipped out of bed and went to the kitchen phone, calling the Four Seasons to make a brunch reservation. A grand gesture, to be sure, but one that seemed called for, one that seemed like the appropriate capper to a perfect night.

He kissed Sandy lightly on the forehead. "Come on, sleepyhead. I've made reservations for brunch at the Four Seasons."

Sandy, who was not a morning person, did not seem pleased. "Are you out of your mind?"

"I know it's expensive, and I know I'm a schoolteacher, but I still have a few dollars socked away from my game-show days. It'll be fun."

"And what do you expect me to wear? The same clothes I wore last night?"

In his romance-addled state, Perry hadn't given much thought to wardrobe, but he recovered quickly.

"I love what you wore last night. You looked perfect."

Sandy had worn black jeans and a white cotton shirt—a man's shirt, most likely—but she had looked smashing.

"This is stupid."

"Please . . ."

It wasn't as if Sandy's previous relationships had worked out so well, and a voice in her head urged her to agree, rather than do anything that would derail this budding relationship.

"I have to shower," she said. "I really do. That's just a given. Wearing yesterday's clothes is one thing, but I'm not putting them on this body until it's clean."

All the L.A. hotels served brunch, but only the Four Seasons had one good enough to drag locals from their king-sized beds and Sony Wega TVs earlyish on a Sunday. The food was excellent, and there were always enough stars staying at the hotel to make it a bit of a special occasion. If it was good enough for Liam Neeson and Leonardo DiCaprio—the first two familiar faces Sandy and Perry saw when they sat down—it was good enough for the rest of upper Los Angeles.

It was hard for Sandy to relax. She didn't like wearing day-old clothing, and she could tell by the way Perry was looking at her that something was amiss with her hair. Of course, something was *always* amiss with her hair—it was so light and thin that it ignored normal physical forces, like gravity, but succumbed to unlikely ones, like noise. Tim claimed that talking too loudly could actually rearrange Sandy's hair. What made it worse was that Perry suffered from serious hair issues. For a guy with a normal head of hair, he certainly had cornered the market on hair-rejuvenation products—she had found four in the shower and three more on the bathroom shelf. Maybe that's why this relationship was meant to be, she thought. Finally, with Perry's guidance, Sandy would find a way to give her hair body.

The third, fourth, fifth, and sixth faces Perry recognized at the Four Seasons were more disconcerting. There was Alex, a student from his English class at Crosswinds, and three other Crosswinds boys, including Matt, another of his students. Four fourteen-year-old boys having brunch by themselves at the Four Seasons, their plates piled greedily high with food, as if they were conducting a taste test of every item the hotel offered. They were noisy, too. Perry heard them before he saw them. Everyone in the room seemed aware of the boys who brunch.

"Who are they?" asked Sandy, who picked up on Perry's interest.

"Crosswinds boys—two of them are my students."

"And they're having brunch. How charming," said Sandy sarcastically.

Alex noticed Perry right away, and he shot over to the table with alarming speed. "It's Perry!" he said, causing every head within a twenty-yard distance to turn. He put up his hand for a high five. Perry feebly obliged.

"Look over there," said Alex, pointing in an overly dramatic fashion to the buffet line where the omelette chef stood. "Go to him. He's my man. He's the best omelette chef in this place. You stay away from the others. We come here all the time, and believe me, he's the best."

"Will do," said Perry.

"I'm going to hit the rest room. See you later," said Alex. Mercifully, he was gone.

"He's intense," said Sandy.

"Oh, very. That's him being mellow," explained Perry.

He watched as, one by one, each of the members of the boys who brunch filed to the men's room, leaving their half-eaten stacks of food to wait.

Perry was intrigued. "I'll be right back."

He followed the boys into the rest room. It was empty. He

ran some water, kept his eye on the stalls, and listened intently. He heard giggling and coughing and, looking in the mirror, watched as a bong was passed underneath one stall onto the next. The smell of pot mingled with disinfectant. Perry bolted before he could be caught.

"They're in there taking bong hits," he whispered to Sandy, whose eyes popped wide open.

"Do they know you know?"

"I don't think so," he said. "I'm just going to pretend I never went in there. I don't want to deal with this when I'm still so new on the job."

One by one, the boys filed back to the table and continued their eat-a-thon. Now they were even louder than before.

By the time they were done, the Four Seasons had clearly lost money on the four boys, who had eaten enough food for a table of ten. But it made money on Sandy, who grabbed a bagel and some fruit from the buffet table and then feigned satisfaction. Even Perry didn't eat enough to justify the cost.

"See you in class, Perry," shouted Alex as the boys left. Perry managed a weak wave.

"Can you imagine bringing a bong to brunch at the Four Seasons?" asked Sandy. "I've done some outrageous things, but that one seems over the edge."

"Oh, absolutely," said Perry. "I want to shrug and say, 'Kids today,' but I can't. I'd sound like my dad. It makes me feel too old."

Instead, he and Sandy just shook their heads, feeling very much like fully grown adults.

# Walking the Dog

**Simon James sat in** his large office with its temporary furniture and unobstructed view of the most boring part of Culver City and indulged in his weekly guilty pleasure. The *New York Observer* and the *New York Press* had arrived, weeks late, as usual, but still nothing vindicated Simon's decision to remain in Los Angeles more than reading the rantings of cranky losers who took themselves way too seriously and had far too many opinions. New Yorkers got upset about things that Angelenos wouldn't give a second thought to, let alone let loose with some overly intellectualized screed. There wasn't one writer at the *New York Press* who could walk past a funeral without turning it into six thousand self-indulgent words (seven thousand if they could somehow include a gratuitous attack on another writer). L.A. was a much saner way to live.

Yet, these same losers looked west and thought Simon was a loser—that was, if they even remembered who Simon was at all. That's why Simon so rarely ventured back to New York. What was the point of going to Elaine's if you were just going to be ignored? No one went there for the food.

That's why Simon had been so eager to take the *Hollywood Today* job. All he needed was a touch of those Internet riches, just a one-paragraph mention in the *Wall Street Journal* or on *Medianews.org* that he had reaped a tremendous windfall and he could return to Elaine's a victor. IPOs did more than make you rich. They provided vindication in abundance.

Sadly, Simon was not feeling vindicated. Synergistic Enterprises, *Hollywood Today*'s parent, which had been in the vanguard of New Media was once again ahead of the curve: It was the first to start tightening its financial belt.

"The conventional wisdom right now," Spencer Sowa, Synergistic's twenty-four-year-old president, had told Simon the day before, "is that content sites have a future, but not a particularly bright financial one. Ad dollars are being spread too thin; no one will fork over any money at all for a subscription site. And besides, every magazine and newspaper in the country is already flaunting their own Web sites. We'll do okay on *Hollywood Today*, but it'll never have the type of profit margins an e-commerce site will have. Synergistic will still do content. I like content. Content is great—in its place. But I like money more."

"Certainly there must be something I can do to help this company grow and justify my profit participation," Simon had said with just a tinge of desperation.

Spencer strolled around his office playing with a yo-yo, shaking his head. He wore a T-shirt with splatters of tomato sauce on it. He had missed a patch shaving. He had a large zit on the side of his nose. His contact lenses were uncomfortable and made him blink constantly.

"Is there something we can sell on *Hollywood Today* that would make sense?" asked Simon. "Collectibles? Movie memorabilia?"

Spencer almost clipped Simon's head trying an around-the-world with the yo-yo.

"Yo-yos are so random," he mused. "Did you know that I once bounced a Ping-Pong ball against my office wall for four hours without stopping? It was very intense."

"I feel as if you brought me in under false pretenses," argued Simon to no one in particular. "I joined this company thinking, as everyone does, that my sacrifices would be rewarded commensurate with others in the industry. I assumed I would be getting stock options in the parent company. Now I find they're with a small subsidiary—*Hollywood Today*—that you think is worthless."

"Yeah, you and everyone else," said Spencer, attempting a walk-the-dog. "But I'm not giving away stock options to people who aren't growing the business. That just wouldn't make sense."

"I'm a man with a lot of experience and many contacts," countered Simon. "Tell me something I can do and I'll do it. This is obviously very important to me."

Spencer stopped and stared. "I'm trying to figure out if your greed is useful to me," he said flatly. "Otherwise, it's just a turnoff."

"Let's pretend for the moment it's useful," said Simon.

"And what if you don't have the stomach for what I need?" asked Spencer playfully.

"Okay, let's pretend I do," said Simon. "What do you have to lose?"

Spencer walked around the office, playing with the yo-yo.

"You have a writer who works for you, Tim Newman. . . ."

Simon nodded.

"Do you think he'd listen to you?"

"I believe so, yes."

"Then here's my proposition. The IPO will happen in a few months, and in order for Synergistic to be at full operation on the Web, I need something. I've been trying to get it, but I've hit a roadblock. You and your colleague can help."

"I think you'll find that Tim is as open as I am to cooperating," said Simon. "He has options, too—and I'm sure he'd like them to be worth something."

"Remember when I asked you to get that information on Tim's father and the Honda dealership he owned?"

Simon remembered, but he was having trouble making the connection.

"Let me ask you a question," said Spencer impatiently. "What's the biggest drawback to buying a car on the Web?"

"I don't know," said a befuddled Simon. "Profit margin?"

"Oh please, I just mentioned profit margins and your eyes glazed over," scoffed Spencer. "Don't make me laugh."

"I don't know then."

"People can't test-drive the cars. It's the same problem with clothing on the Web. You can't test the product. And too many people are too decent to go to a brick and mortar dealership, kick the tires, take the test drive, and then walk away, go home, and use the Web. And dealers are too savvy. If they know that a potential pigeon is Web-savvy, they whip out the invoice and convince him he's not going to get a better deal from us. So here's the challenge: How can we make more buyers comfortable with spending tens of thousands on the Web without risking losing them to a real dealer?"

"How?"

"A test-drive center. A centrally located old-fashioned car lot—one that has one each of every car we're likely to sell. We'll have them all over the country. But this car market is huge, and it's Web-friendly. Go to our test-drive center—no salesman will hassle you, because *there are no salesmen.* Just the mere existence of the place will put buyers' minds at ease. It's genius.

"I need that dealership. It's the only privately owned dealership in the area—everything else is part of a big chain. It's a great location and it comes with all the stupid government licenses and paperwork. If Synergistic is going to be a one-stop e-commerce and content Web company, I need Newman Super Honda. I can't sell cars unless I have a licensed dealership—it's the law. Right now, I can match buyers up with willing car dealers, but they take the big profits. That's very yesterday. I don't want to be a matchmaker anymore. I want to get laid. If I own a dealership, I can get the license and I can build my test-drive center. Do you get it?"

"Where do I come in?"

"See if you can't get Tim to talk some sense into his father's thick head. His partners are greedy, like you, and willing to sell out their partnership for shares in Synergistic. But Tim's father is holding firm. Do something about that."

"How?"

Spencer laughed. "If it was easy, it would have been done by now. And if it had been that easy, it wouldn't be worth stock options, now would it? If you want your stock options to be in Synergistic instead of in modestly valued *Hollywood Today* stock, you two will figure it out. That's called earning your money."

He spun the yo-yo and did the baby-in-the-cradle, snapping the yo-yo back into his hand with a flourish. Without another word, he walked out the door.

## The Newmans Know How to Party

**Ann and Syd sat** on their king-sized bed like two little kids, feet dangling over the edge like two children whose feet couldn't touch the floor. They sat in silence, gently holding hands. That's what happens when you turn your party over to professionals. You're just a couple of meddlesome, highly strung Valley Jews who get in the way. The caterer had made that very clear as he and his team set up. Slightly slow to pick up on the hint, Ann and Syd finally retreated to their bedroom with nothing to do, too anxious to talk and too superfluous to do anything else.

Ann was eager. The minutes dragged by slowly. She could hardly wait for the party to begin. Syd was apprehensive. The party was hurtling at him like a meteorite. If only he had time to get out of the way.

Ann had nearly run out of patience by the time the caterer rapped on the door. Syd couldn't figure out what the rush was.

"Come," said the caterer, an authoritative frat boy who barked orders to his crew of illegals in fluent Spanish. "Take a look."

"It looks wonderful," gushed Ann. Indeed, she wouldn't have recognized her own backyard. Fifteen tables with brightly colored tablecloths and dozens of glowing luminarias occupied the large lawn. Buffet tables and a margarita bar were perched on the covered pool. White twinkle lights were strewn in the tall hedge that served as the back fence. Off in the corner, where no one could see him, was the disc jockey and his traveling mammoth speakers, plus a list of approved songs that had been drawn largely from TV commercials, especially ones for the Gap and Banana Republic. The goal, after all, was to recreate the ambience of the Pottery Barn. Ann always felt happy in the Pottery Barn.

Perry and Sandy were the first to arrive. That was part of Perry's scheme. He wanted Sandy to meet his parents, and vice versa; and he didn't want to miss the look on his parents' face when Tim and Antonio arrived.

They joined Ann and Syd to test the margarita bar. They occupied a series of varying stops along the Southern California fashion continuum: Ann in her sharply tailored suit, Syd in his style-free khakis and boxy Brooks Brothers cotton shirt, Perry in jeans with the standard T-shirt and pullover sweater combo, and Sandy dressed in that artist/gypsy/hippie ensemble that somehow worked—and even made Ann a little envious. Perry had created a set of expectations with his previous girlfriends, the ones who were chosen for something more practical than romance. It was clear to both Ann and Syd that, with Sandy, Perry was experimenting with a different direction.

"How did you two meet?" Ann asked Sandy as Perry and Syd engaged in one of their exclusionary guy talks.

"I'm a friend of Tim's, actually," said Sandy. "We work right next to each other. He's probably one of my best friends."

"And one of your least punctual friends," said Ann, nervously scanning the empty backyard for signs of Tim.

"If he's as prompt tonight as he is at work, we'll see him around ten," said Sandy.

"He's not a morning person, that's for sure," said Ann. "None of the men in the family are, but Tim might take it to an extreme."

At that point, the real guests started arriving, and Ann and Syd slipped into host mode, moving as a unit to the front door.

"You *are* a Valley boy," said Sandy as Perry gave her a tour of the family estate, with all its Valley tract-home touches—including an oddly shaped multipurpose room at the top of the stairs.

"You can take the boy out of the Valley, but . . ." Perry laughed. "Deep down, I'm always going to think a wet bar is really cool."

That gave Perry something in common with the rest of the guests. The Newman family social circle also appreciated the good life the Valley had to offer, an appreciation not only of wet bars and pool skimmers but of Red Lobster restaurants and miniature golf courses, as well. They were not so much friends as clones—a group of acquaintances bound together by their striking similarities and their surprising lack of differences. Indeed, every couple present had kids Perry's age whom Perry and Tim had grown up with, and every conversation Sandy witnessed consisted of Perry giving his current résumé, Tim's current résumé, and a promise to call young David, Micki, Jim, Linda, Mark, Susan—whomever—for lunch very soon.

As much as possible, Sandy and Perry tried to be moving targets, eating standing up, always appearing as if they were on their way to join someone, somewhere, avoiding as many conversations as possible. That strategy gave them the added benefit of overhearing golden nuggets of conversation on the fly.

"It's not really a face-lift. It's done with lasers."

"This food is good, but I don't understand why Ann didn't call Art's. Art's knows how to cater."

"It's cancer. I feel so bad for her, because once they open you up, the air causes the cancer to spread. And then you're gone."

"Jury duty? You must want to kill yourself."

"No, Perry's the straight one who used to be successful. Tim's the gay one who can't find himself."

For Ann, things were going fantastically. Even Syd had to admit that as parties go, this one was survivable. Amid the marathon of schmoozing, they were both acutely aware that Tim was a no-show. That wasn't like Tim at all.

The food choices were limited and the Corona was gone by the time Tim and Antonio arrived. Late entrances are always high-profile, and this one was higher than most. Tim had gone to extra lengths for the occasion, upgrading his wardrobe to more of a Politix chic. And Antonio was instantly recognizable, even if you didn't watch the WB. There was an aura of gay glamour around them that almost everyone noticed.

"You look very nice," Sandy said to Tim. "I feel like I created a monster."

"Why are you so fucking late?" asked Perry. "If I left you alone in this crowd, you'd have a fit."

"It's not my fault," whispered Tim, leaning close to his brother's ear. "We've been parked down the street for a goddamn hour while Antonio fought with his agent over some producer's credit on a TV movie. He's so ambitious, it's frightening."

Ann and Syd descended on the boys like SCUD missiles. There was nothing more normal than the four Newmans together—it had been that way for twenty-six years—and yet there was something disconcerting about the four Newmans plus two. No one could relate the way they usually did, but everyone felt the need to pretend that things were perfect. After all, they wouldn't be the four Newmans forever. Eventually, the boys—well, Perry—would pair off for good, and start families—or whatever—of their own. And who knew what loomed in Tim's future. Ann tried to imagine Antonio at Thanksgiving dinner. She tried to picture Sandy opening Christmas presents in the living room. Or Hanukkah, or Easter, or Passover—any of the multitude of holidays the Newmans were known to celebrate. But the images were incomplete and distorted, like a defective videotape from Blockbuster.

Late that night, after the caterers had vanished, magically taking all of the trash with them, and the guests had all been walked to their cars, Ann and Syd ended the event very much as they had started it, sitting on the edge of the bed.

"Sandy seemed nice," offered Syd.

"Yes," said Ann. "She was a pleasant surprise, not at all what I expected."

"We had a celebrity at the party. That was unusual."

"Tim was full of surprises tonight, wasn't he?" Ann sighed. "Antonio was a surprise, yes. I never imagined Tim with anyone like Antonio. Did you?"

"I'll tell you something even more disturbing," confided Syd.

"I don't think I want to know."

"I saw the new car."

"How bad is it?" asked Ann.

"If Tim's new car were a person, it would be Antonio," said Syd. "Antonio is the human version of a BMW 318ti."

"Oh Tim," moaned Ann, burying her head in her hands.

"I know," agreed Syd. "And it's only a four-cylinder. A BMW with four cylinders. How stupid can you be?"

## "Come on Down!"

**The first time Perry** saw his classroom at Crosswinds, he was thrilled. A glistening white board with a rainbow of dry erase markers, a thirty-six-inch TV suspended from the ceiling, with WebTV, a VCR, and a DVD player. Perry loved technology.

"Let's talk about the role superstition plays in *To Kill a Mockingbird,*" Perry urged his class.

Silence.

"Do any of the characters strike you as superstitious?" he asked.

Nothing.

"Okay, let's try it this way—are the Hot Steams in chapter four anything to be afraid of?"

The silence was punctured by a most unexpected sound.

*"Jerry, Jerry, Jerry—"* The TV had mysteriously turned on and Jerry Springer was displayed in all his intellectual glory. Perry walked over and pushed the power button.

"See, the Hot Steams are spirits, and apparently, our TV is haunted."

"Jem and Scout are afraid of the Hot Steams," offered Caitlin.

"That's true," said Perry. "What do they think will happen to them?"

*"Come on down!"* The TV had turned back on, and Bob Barker was getting ready to greet another contestant.

"This is odd," said Perry and he walked toward the TV. Before he could get to it, the channels suddenly starting changing. Bob Barker gave way to Oprah, who led to the return of Jerry, who lingered briefly before Judge Judy made an appearance. She was quickly replaced by the HBO logo.

"This is really odd," mused Perry. He yanked the plug from the wall. "I'll report this to the office at lunch."

So much for the Hot Steams and irrational fears of haints, Mrs. Dubose, and Boo Radley. Perry's class was too distracted by the haunted TV set to do any work. Perry kept the TV unplugged during his next two classes.

Wednesday was Perry's Lunch Day. Lunch Day was a Crosswinds tradition, intended to help students and teachers interact in a more casual environment. One day a month, a teacher was "encouraged" (which was the Crosswinds version of *assigned*) to join the students in the yard during lunch to mingle and talk. "Teachers spend too much time with teachers," intoned Bob Parrish. "You can learn more from students than you can from teachers."

When he got to the yard, clutching the brown-bag lunch he had made that morning, Perry was surprised at how empty it was. It seemed like only a few of the students were at the tables, and they were younger. Perry didn't know any of them.

Even confusion didn't hamper Perry's appetite, so he staked out a shady table and sat down to begin lunch. He was halfway through his sandwich when the yard filled with kids.

Only a teacher would be so nerdy as to bring his own lunch, so the students flocked to the food-service window and a catering truck that was parked at the curb.

"Oh, Perry—is this your Lunch Day?" asked Caitlin sweetly. "You should have told us. We could have told you how to get real food." She sat down opposite him with a small sushi tray and a diet Coke.

Alex was next, carrying two giant slices of pepperoni pizza and two diet Cokes. "Here," he said, shoving a can toward Perry. "I bought you a Coke."

"That's very nice of you," said Perry, feeling painfully unhip with his brown bag. "How much is it? I'll pay you back."

"No prob," said Alex. "You can get the next one."

Soon Perry was surrounded by a number of his students. As out of place as he felt, they seemed perfectly relaxed, as if joining a teacher for lunch was just a typical day. Other than the free Coke, they didn't seem to treat Perry much like an outsider at all.

"Why was everyone so late for lunch?" asked Perry. "It was empty out here."

"Didn't you hear?" said Caitlin. "Danny's dad brought in a rough cut of the new *Ocean's Eleven* for Communication Arts and we all went to the auditorium to watch it. George Clooney is so cute, for an old guy."

"The movie wasn't bad," interjected Alex. "But the music stunk. I mean, even for a rough cut, you'd think they'd come up with better than that crap."

"It doesn't matter," said an exasperated Caitlin. "They'll

put the real music in later. I just hate when there are no sound effects."

"I think it'll do okay," offered Alex. "Maybe not a big opening, but it'll have legs overseas and in home video."

"When does it come out?" asked Perry.

"Not until Christmas," said Caitlin. "They have plenty of time."

"So, you have a really cute girlfriend," said Alex, changing the subject.

Perry waited for someone to answer. Finally, it dawned on him that Alex was talking to him.

"Me?" said a flustered Perry.

"Yeah, remember, I saw you two at the Four Seasons. Besides, you ate at my dad's table at the fund-raiser. He said she was really cute and that he liked you a lot."

"That's very nice of him. I liked him, too."

"He's cool," agreed Alex. "He's, like, my best friend."

The conversations that surrounded Perry continued at a frantic pace, with almost every student doing his or her best to keep the lone teacher included. These kids have a confidence and poise I never had at their age, thought Perry. I'm not so sure I have it now.

As kids wandered away from the table, Perry soon found himself alone with Alex.

"Have I ever shown you my watch?" asked Alex.

Perry shook his head.

"Look." Alex stuck his wrist under Perry's nose. It was an elaborate Casio with a numeric keypad and several large buttons.

"What does it do? Logarithms?"

"Better than that." Alex smiled. "It's a TV remote control. It'll work on any set, once you figure out the code."

It took a few seconds for the impact of Alex's confession to sink in.

"I take it you've figured out the code for the TVs here at school," he said.

"You bet," said Alex without a shred of concern. "That's why I bought you a Coke. I owed you."

"Yeah, I guess you did," said Perry. At least the classroom is not haunted, he thought.

"We're still friends, right?" asked Alex.

"Sure, why not?" replied Perry, somewhat impressed at Alex's chutzpah.

"Great!" said Alex, as if he'd expected no other response. "See you tomorrow."

And to think that the other teachers dreaded Lunch Day.

## PowerHair.doc

**"Now you've met Mom** and Dad," said Tim, eager to do a party postmortem with Sandy. "Does that explain Perry and me?"

"Nothing explains *you,*" said Sandy. "But your parents seem normal enough."

"Even Mom?" asked Tim, slumping in the guest chair in Sandy's cube.

"Well, there might have been a bit of self-absorption there," admitted Sandy. "But I'll bet she was a really devoted mom. I'll bet you two were spoiled rotten and the entire focus of her existence. Without you and Perry, she's just lost, that's all. She'll never find a project that interesting again."

"That's pretty close to the truth," agreed Tim. "She was

never happier than when we were little. She's just in limbo until Perry gives her grandchildren. Wink, wink. Nudge, nudge."

"Oh shut up."

"I just believe in full disclosure. She wasn't examining you as merely daughter-in-law potential this weekend. She was pondering how much you'd let her baby-sit your kids."

"Yes, Mr. Full Disclosure. The man who won't even tell his parents that he's gay."

"I'll tell them. Eventually."

"Eventually? Do you think they don't suspect?"

"I *know* they suspect. They never hint about grandkids with me. And once, Mom asked if I'd like to be buried with them. They were buying a cemetery plot, and they were thinking of accommodations for three, not two. And not four. Perry was on his own."

"Good God, what did you say?"

"I told her I wanted to be cremated and have my ashes scattered in the fountain at Universal City Walk," said Tim. "She never mentioned it again."

"So why don't you just talk about it? It's clearly not an issue with them. They certainly didn't seem unnerved by Antonio."

"I've never found the right time. I didn't tell them when I was in high school, because I kept thinking it would change. It was too soon. I wasn't sure myself. Then later, I was too self-conscious. Every time I went somewhere with a guy, I thought they'd be thinking I was having sex. And that just creeped me out. Now it's almost too late. I mean, why now? Why didn't I tell them before? It's almost insulting."

"And they never asked?"

"Nope, not ever. Probably for all the same reasons I never told them."

"Why did you tell Perry?"

"I don't recall ever telling him, to tell you the truth. He just always knew. We still don't talk about it much."

"How did I get involved with you two, anyway?"

"A little late to ask that one, I'm afraid," said Tim. He stood up on the chair and looked across the room to Simon's glassed-in office. "Have you noticed that Simon's office door has been closed for days now? He just sits in there and broods."

"I noticed. What do you think it is? Is he sick?"

"I don't know, but I need to spring something on him, and I've been waiting for the right time."

Sandy stood up and peered over her cubicle wall. Simon was turned in his big swivel chair, with his back to the glass, staring out the window at downtown Culver City.

"I'm trying something different for my column. Instead of a profile."

"What is it?" asked Sandy.

"Sort of a humor thing. You can read it, if you want. It's under 'PowerHair.doc' in my folder. But I'm going back to work. I don't want to watch while you read it."

It didn't take Sandy long to read the thousand words.

"Have you gone insane?" she said aloud, sitting at her computer, knowing that Tim was just half a wall away, waiting.

"I'll take that as a negative," said Tim, crestfallen.

"Are you crazy?" she repeated. "Are you attempting complete and total self-annihilation?"

"Is it that bad?" Tim's voice was meek. "You didn't think it was funny at all?"

Sandy was exasperated. She stood and looked over at Tim.

"It's funny. It might even be too funny. But do you realize what you're doing?"

"Making people laugh?"

"You're making fun of hair in Hollywood. You're making

fun of Ron Howard and his baseball cap. You claim Brian Grazer taunted him by spiking his hair. You list every man in Hollywood who dyes his hair. Garry Shandling? Poor Martin Short—as if he doesn't have enough problems. No one even knows who Ian Ziering is anymore. You talk about David Kelley's bald spot!"

"So do you! You're obsessed with it."

"I talk about it. I don't write about it. I have no desire to have every flack in this city hate me."

"That bad, huh?"

"Show it to Simon. Let him decide."

"Do you think he'll hate it?" asked Tim.

"Look at him right now," commanded Sandy. Tim stood up and looked toward Simon's office. He was still leaning back in his chair, gazing out the window.

"What do you see?" asked Sandy.

"A depressed old man in a nice office," said Tim.

"I see a man with a bald spot the size of a yarmulke. How do you think he'll respond?"

Tim looked again. Funny how that fact had slipped his mind. Maybe Sandy was right. Maybe he did have a death wish.

## Starbucks-o-rama

**Syd should have known better.** When he told Ann, "Meet me at the Starbucks on Ventura Boulevard," he should have been more specific. Of course, now that he was in his third Starbucks, scanning the tables for his wife, he realized that Ventura Boulevard alone had forty-seven Starbucks, running the whole length of it. Even in this section of Sherman Oaks, there were more Starbucks than gas stations, one every few blocks. When he added in the Coffee Beans, Tanners, and Peets, Syd came to two inescapable conclusions: One, he was living in a highly caffeinated world, full of hyper, teeth-grinding people who were both highly tolerant of acid and had lots of free time. Two, he might never find Ann.

Indeed, finding Ann was a challenge. It wasn't until his fifth

Starbucks that he found her, well into her decaf Tiazzi and biscotti.

"Do you know how many Starbucks I've been to?" asked Syd, panting, as he collapsed in the chair.

"I always come to this one. You know that."

How was I supposed to know? he wondered. He was at work every day, and for him, Ann's daytime comings and goings were mysterious. And exhausting, apparently. Ann often marveled how she had the stamina to do it all. Whatever *all* was.

"We have a problem," said Syd, attacking the issue directly. Ann sat up straight, fearing the worst.

"The partners want to sell the dealership, and it's not a good deal for us. An Internet company needs the license and the land, but not me or the staff. They want to give us all stock and send us on our way."

"Internet stock?" Ann was intrigued.

"I'm convinced it sounds better than it is. We all get stock, which on paper is a fair—maybe even generous—price for the dealership. But we can't sell it for one year. If the stock goes up in that time, we're set for life. If it goes down, whatever plans we have for a pleasant retirement go out the window. The dealership is our retirement account. I always knew that when the time came, I could sell my share and we'd glide off into our golden years. But I always assumed I'd get cash, not stock in some fly-by-night company."

"Poor Syd," said Ann, reaching across the table. "No wonder you've been so distracted. Why didn't you tell me?"

"You had other things going on. The party, that secession thing . . ."

"I wish you had told me. I feel stupid talking about my silly little projects when you're in the middle of this."

"Well, next time," said Syd with a laugh.

"What are you going to do?"

"Divide and conquer. At least that's what I've been trying. Brian DeSalvo got the partners worked up with dreams of Internet riches. I've been talking to them individually, trying to show them that they could lose everything."

"Is it working?"

"Not really. I talk to them and they go home, turn on the news, and see another Internet company go public and everyone get rich. They want some of that."

"Don't you?"

"I'd love it. But I'm not at an age where I can gamble. This company—it's called Synergistic—has existed for about fifteen minutes. They started a bunch of Web sites and caused a stir. But they've not even come close to making a profit. They manage to lose money on everything they do, but investors keep giving them more money, driving up the stock.

"So now they have this stock that they've managed to inflate to some astronomical heights. And they know it's basically worthless—or, at the very least, worth a fraction of what it's trading for. They have to strike while they can, and take this inflated stock and gobble up as many businesses as possible. But eventually, it has to catch up with them. More and more of these stocks are plummeting. A lot of these Web sites have already crashed and burned."

"I feel so bad for you," said Ann.

"You should feel bad for *us*. It's our money."

"Oh, Syd darling. You've taken such good care of me—of all of us—for so long, I don't even know how to worry. What's the worst that can happen? We'll both get jobs. Wouldn't that be a hoot? Imagine how much fun the boys would have if I got a *real* job? It might be worth it to keep them entertained."

"Well, don't go filling out any applications yet. And let's not tell the boys. But I wanted you to know that it was serious. And that I might be hanging around the house sooner than we expected."

"Oh God." Ann sighed. "Then I'd really have to get a job."

Syd laughed.

"I've spent my entire adult life watching you," said Ann, "and I've never seen you come close to failure. You're the smartest, most resilient man I know. It's been intimidating. Not just for me but, I think, for the boys, too. We've all been in awe of you, even if you don't know it. I can't conceive of you not emerging triumphant. You always pull it off, and you know it."

At the car, Ann gave Syd a hug and sent him on back to the wars. She had meant what she said. Everyone believes in something, and Ann believed with religious fervor that Syd would always take care of her.

If anything, Ann felt bad that she couldn't be of more help. All this talk about stock and the Internet made her feel inadequate, and right at the time she should be there to help and advise her husband. But how could she have helped when she'd been so busy with her counseling and CUSS and the party? This whole Internet thing had slipped by her, like understanding the situation in Ireland or learning to do the electric slide. Now her inattention had come back to haunt her. It was time to take action, and she knew what action she could take. She took out her cell phone and called Tim.

"Sweetheart, I need you," she said. "I need to get a computer and get on the Internet. This whole Internet thing has passed me by, and I want to understand it. Could you get me a cheap computer and set me up on the Internet?"

"Sure, it's easy," said Tim. "I could pick up a computer at Best Buy and have you up and running in an hour."

"Could you do it soon?" she asked. "It's important. And now that I think of it, don't make the computer too cheap. I like those colored ones you see on the commercials. Maybe a blue or a green one, if they have it. Is that okay?"

## Simon Unveiled

**The IM flashed across** Tim's screen.

> **Simon825:** Do you want to come in and talk about Power Hair?

"Simon wants to talk to me about Power Hair," Tim said to Sandy.

"Oh, good luck," said Sandy. "It was nice knowing you."

> **TimTimTim:** Be right there.

Tim took two deep breaths and walked to Simon's office, not sure what to expect.

"I see you're branching out," said Simon. "Getting away from those chat and chews."

"I thought I might," said Tim. "What do you think?"

"It's very funny. I think you should go with it."

Tim waited. "That's it?" he asked.

"Why? What were you expecting?"

"Sandy thought I was committing professional suicide, that I'd never have lunch in this town again."

"You'll go through a rough patch, but I assumed you knew that and were willing to accept the consequences. It'll pass. Publicists have short memories and no scruples. If you're useful to them, they'll forget this ever happened. Then they'll just turn on you again. It'll happen over and over, if you stay with this."

"Oh, I intend to stay with it," said Tim. "This is the most fun I've ever had."

"Don't you sometimes think it would be more fun to be on the other side?" asked Simon wistfully. "Rather that live in fear of *them*, would you rather be the one getting angry? Wouldn't you rather be the one written about?"

"Move over to upper Los Angeles, you mean? I didn't know that was an option."

"What if you had so much money you never had to work again? What if you could spend the rest of your life doing exactly what you want to do, not working to make a living or to please a boss?"

Tim was under the impression that he was doing what he wanted to do, but if hanging out with Antonio had taught him anything, it was that there were lots of people in Los Angeles who had a lot more money than Tim had. That's why signing on with *Hollywood Today* had been such a great move.

"You know those stock options you have?"

Tim nodded.

"They're worthless."

Tim felt deflated. His eyes moistened. He had tried not to think about the stock options—he kept telling himself that he had bought a lottery ticket that might pay off big, but more likely wouldn't. Still, in his dreams and plans, he saw himself existing at a comfort level far above the one he currently occupied.

"Worthless? As in zero?" he stammered.

"Yes," said Simon defiantly. "At the moment, they're worth nothing. Zip."

"At the moment?"

Simon stood up walked over to his window, avoiding eye contact.

"I'm going to tell you something I've never told anyone else. I hardly even allow this thought to exist in my head. Do you know how much I hate my job?"

"I didn't know you hated your job at all."

"It's not just my job," Simon continued. "It's this entire industry. An industry full of people smart enough to think and write well, yet not smart enough to make real money. Smart enough to influence the world, but too stupid to turn that talent into a nice house, a nice car, a big stock portfolio."

He faced Tim. "Let me ask you something. Do you think you're any dumber than any of the people you've been profiling?"

"Of course not. They're actors. They're supposed to be dumb."

"And what about the screenwriters and directors and studio heads? Are they smarter than you?"

Tim was flummoxed. "I don't know. Maybe, maybe not. I haven't thought about it that much."

"Do you know how many millions of dollars a Lynda Obst

or Brian Grazer has? David Kelley? Steven Bochco? Sherry Lansing? Do you have any idea the level of respect they garner in the industry?"

Tim assumed that as high-powered and successful producers, they were both well paid and well respected.

"How many millions do you have? How many do I have?"

"I'm guessing that neither one of us has millions," offered Tim.

"It's bigger than that," insisted Simon. "I've spent my entire career with my nose pressed against the glass. I've watched a bunch of idiots far less intelligent and talented than I am—and I'm being realistic here, Tim, not conceited—make fortunes. Become famous. Get written about by people like *us.*"

"What are you trying to tell me? Are you firing me? Should I go home and write a screenplay?"

"I don't want you to make the same mistakes I made. I want you to have enough money in the bank so that you can have nice things and earn the respect of the people in this town. I don't want you to have to beg and scheme the way I have. You've seen my car. . . ."

"The Lincoln. It's a nice car."

"Do you honestly think I could afford that? That's not mine. It's a trade-out—we run ads on the Web site and I get a free lease. Most of the ads are like that. That's how I travel. That's how I eat."

"My head is swimming," said Tim. "This is the opposite of everything you've ever said to me."

"I'm very sorry I lied to you," Simon said. "But I had pride. I knew inside that I had made a career mistake. Admitting that, even to you, is very hard."

"You've certainly given me something to think about," said Tim, who stood up, ready to return to his pathetic career, his sorry little cubicle, and his doomed life.

"Let me give you one more thing to think about," said

Simon. "You have it within your reach to change things, to have enough money so that you can have some self-respect."

"I do?"

"Those stock options don't have to be worthless. Synergistic is expanding, and if they're able to pull off one important deal, our stock options could make us rich."

"What's the deal?" Tim continued standing.

"Synergistic wants to buy your father's car dealership. All the partners have agreed, only your father is fighting it. Talk to him. Make him realize what a great opportunity this is for everyone—for his partners, for himself. And make sure he understands what it can mean to you. Every father wants to help his children. And it's not only good for us; it's good for him, too."

Tim had never felt more confused. He left Simon and went straight out the front door, walking the streets of Culver City to clear his head. There had been too much going on—landing a job, getting the column, having stock options, meeting Antonio, buying the BMW, watching Perry falter. It should have been the most exciting time of his twenty-six years. But Tim wasn't excited. He wasn't even happy. He felt the way he always knew he'd feel if success struck—like a fraud. Back in junior high school, when he first worked on the school newspaper, he'd known he wanted to be a newspaper reporter. Not a TV news guy—that would be too flashy. He'd felt content even then with his behind-the-scenes role, the guy who lived vicariously through the accomplishments of others. The more he walked and thought, the more he feared that he had somehow strayed off the right path and was being punished for it. Or maybe he had just been a underachiever for so long that he was ill at ease with all this success. But was dating Antonio a sign of success? Was the BMW? What about selling his dad down the river?

Finally, as it grew darker, he went to the parking lot, got his car, and went home, not returning to the office until well past midnight, when everyone else was gone.

## The Carson Gymnasium

**One of the most** seductive things about Crosswinds was the country club atmosphere—the large grassy areas shaded by big leafy trees. The pond and waterfall, where students could go to contemplate (or smoke or make out or hide). The bungalow-style classrooms had wide windows, air conditioning, carpeting, and, of course, state-of-the-art electronics. No institutional green walls. No bells ringing at the end of class. No chain-link fences. If it'd had a golf course and a good restaurant, they could have turned the whole thing into a resort and made real money.

Even parent-teacher conferences had a casual vibe, like old friends dropping by for a visit. Crosswinds was one big happy family. As headmaster, Bob Parrish was the father of one wing of the family. As the most generous and visible parent, Rubin Carson was the father of the other. In a public school, Bob would have been king. At Crosswinds, it was hard to tell who wielded more power.

Yet Rubin and his wife could not have been more gregarious and seemingly down-to-earth when they showed up to discuss Alex's progress with Perry. Sure, they had met over dinner at the fund-raiser, but Perry was still surprised when Rubin greeted him with a gigantic hug.

"Tell me about my Alex," he instructed.

"Alex's a live one," said Perry. "When I need to get discussion going, I call on him first. He's bright, he's witty, he's full of all sorts of outrageous ideas, and he's fearless about expressing them."

The Carsons beamed with pride.

"I'm sure I'm not telling you anything you don't know when I say he's not quite as conscientious with his work. He does maybe half his homework; his test scores are a consistent C. And frankly, he wouldn't do *that* well if he didn't rely on Cliffs Notes, which he waves about unabashedly in class."

Rubin leaned forward. "That was very well put. Let me ask you a question. Have you ever done any writing?"

Perry was not prepared for such a sharp left turn in the conversation. "Actually, I was a writer. I worked on *Boing!* And I even wrote the pilot for *Dire Straights.*"

Rubin turned to his wife. "See, I told you." Then, shifting his focus back to Perry, he said, "I told her after our dinner that I thought you were a writer. I can always tell. I know talent. I have a sixth sense."

Rubin had a salesman's intensity when he spoke. "Why did you leave? Someone with your intelligence should be a show runner. I'm always looking for bright young talent like you."

Briefly, and with a minimum of self-pity, Perry explained

the sad saga of Nancy, Heather, his broken heart, and his broken career.

"I hate that aspect of our business," said Rubin, shaking his head. "I just hate it. But let me tell you—you shouldn't worry. This isn't the time or place, but when this school year is over, you'll come to my office, we'll sit down, and we'll talk about your future. I have a good feeling about you."

"Thank you very much," said Perry. "That's very nice."

"Now," said Rubin. "How can we raise Alex's *C* to an *A*?"

"That might be hard to do," said Perry. "Even if he were to get an *A* on all the work he owes me, he'd only bring himself to a *B*, maybe a *B*-plus."

There was a knock on the door. Bob Parrish opened the door and stuck his head in. "Can I interrupt and say hi?" he asked.

If Perry was surprised by the hug he had received, the embrace Rubin gave Bob was just this side of French kissing. Rubin was a very warm and friendly man.

"I'll let you get back to your meeting with Perry," said Bob. "But when you're done, I want you to stop by the office. I have the blueprints for the new gymnasium"—he turned to Perry and added, "the new *Carson* Gymnasium"—"and I think you'll be very pleased."

"For two million, I should hope so," said Rubin, and the Carsons and Bob enjoyed a hearty laugh.

"Take good care of this man, Perry," said Bob as he left. "We need more families like the Carsons here at Crosswinds."

"I will," volunteered Perry. "I promise."

Rubin turned his attention to the problem at hand, "Here's what I don't understand, Perry. If we can get Alex's grade to *B*-plus, why can't we get it just a notch more and make it an *A*? We're so close. There must be a way."

"Well, yes—that makes sense," said an unsure Perry. "Let

me meet with Alex after school this week and we'll see if we can't work something out. But I can't make promises. There are only a few weeks left, and Alex has a lot to make up."

"Alex won't let you down, Perry. I promise," said Rubin. "But don't you let us down, either. I run my life by a very simple equation: You take care of me and I'll take care of you."

Perry walked the Carsons to the door. Looking across the grassy knoll, he could see the site where the Carson Gymnasium would be erected, a tribute to both the tremendous fortune to be made in sitcoms and to the man who knew how to use that money wisely.

# A Whole New Level of Failure

**For a while, Syd** thought Ann was never going to bed. She had been glued to the new computer since the second Tim had finished setting it up. Ann tackled the world of America Online with the same obsessive enthusiasm she brought to all her projects. She might have come late to the Internet, but she certainly was making up for lost time. With the cordless phone cradled on her shoulder, she called everyone she could think of and had amassed an address book full of E-mail addresses by nightfall. She called Perry and made him go on-line so she could exchange her first instant messages. Like a kid, she was full of wide-eyed wonder and excitement.

"I think I'll buy some tulip bulbs," she said at one point, placing her credit card on the keyboard for easy access. "You like tulip bulbs, don't you?"

"Aren't your eyes tired?" asked Syd, who desperately wanted her to turn off the machine and go to bed.

"Tired?" she answered. "They're burning. They feel like charcoal briquettes. But this is so much fun."

Syd was nervous. Tim had called earlier and said he needed to talk—it was urgent and they needed to talk alone. Tim had never done anything remotely like this before—he was the least melodramatic member of the Newman family. They agreed he'd come by late, after Ann had gone to sleep. But at her current rate, that might be 4:00 A.M. and a dozen books from Amazon.com later.

"Oh, my, did you know you can play hearts with actual people?" said an amazed Ann. "I could do this every day!"

Finally, after a solid hour of playing hearts, Ann signed off.

"I'm exhausted," she complained. "I can't imagine why I'm so tired."

"Hearts can do that to you," said Syd. "You should go to bed."

"Are you coming?" she asked.

"I'll watch a little TV first," he said. "Maybe one of my Carson tapes."

With Ann safely asleep, Syd went downstairs to the den and called Tim. A quick twenty minutes later, Syd heard the BMW pull into the driveway.

Tim was sweaty and disheveled. He seemed slightly winded.

"I don't know how much you know or how much Mom knows, so I thought we better talk privately. I know that you're being pressured to sell the dealership. But here's what you might not know. Synergistic Enterprises, the company that owns *Hollywood Today,* is the same company that wants to buy you out, and, believe it or not, they want me to talk you into going along. It was bizarre. It was like I was being bribed to go against my own father."

"You might not have to talk me into it," said Syd. "I might not have a choice."

"I just want you to know that I don't care what you do. Something is very fishy here. Simon James is one of the best people I've ever met—he's smart; he's worked with every good writer in the country. But something's gone terribly wrong. Either he's not the guy I thought he was or he's gone crazy. He said things that creeped me out today. I feel as if I've been lied to and used. I have a weird feeling, and I wanted to warn you."

"It's an unsavory deal, and it's been handled in an underhanded way," said Syd. "Otherwise, I'd probably be in favor of it. I never intended to sell cars forever."

"You know those stock options I have in *Hollywood Today*? Simon James claims they're worthless."

"I'm sorry to hear that," said Syd, not bothering to add that that was his suspicion about Synergistic's stock, as well.

"I kept asking myself, How could that be?" said Tim, pacing around the den. "We have ads on every page—dozens and dozens of ads. We have really high traffic, so we're delivering eyeballs to those ads."

"Well, it's a start-up," pointed out Syd. "You know how that goes."

"But it made me curious. So I went back to the office tonight and started nosing around when no one was there. I photocopied these for you."

He opened his canvas book bag and produced a sheaf of papers, handing them to Syd.

"They're E-mails, memos, insertion orders, and monthly activity reports."

"So?"

"Hardly any of the ads on the site are paid for. Some are for other divisions of Synergistic, and *Hollywood Today* claims the revenue, but it's money that goes from one pocket of Synergistic to the other. Other ads are trade-outs. We run an ad for a Web site, and, in exchange, they run an ad for us. All those Lincoln ads, for instance. Lincoln doesn't pay, but they give Simon a free car lease. Other ads are almost given away, so the site will look healthy. There's no real money coming in, at least not enough to count."

"How did you find all this out?"

"Simon told me about the Lincoln ads, and it made me curious. We've never had a sales staff the way a magazine does. Everything seemed to be part of the marketing department, and that always confused me. So I went into the office late tonight and snooped around."

"I don't want you getting in trouble on my account," warned Syd.

"Trouble? I have stock options. I'm like a part owner myself. If I don't have a right to this stuff legally, I certainly do morally."

"I'll read these, but I don't know what I can do with them."

"Dad, *Hollywood Today* doesn't make any money and no one ever thought it would. There are memos that say exactly that. It was created to boost Synergistic stock so that Synergistic would look bigger and could buy up other companies without raising money. It's like a con game. Maybe all their sites are run the same way. They've created the illusion of a company, and shareholders are buying into that. Show these to your partners. Tell them what they're getting into."

Tim was so earnest and anxious, Syd wanted to pour him a drink. But Tim was right. If these papers changed only two minds, Syd could keep Newman's Super Honda from being sold.

"If I show these to my partners, word might get out," said Syd. "You might get into trouble."

Tim laughed. "I saw a side of Simon James I didn't much

like today. And for a while, I saw a side of me I didn't much like. Besides, do you know anybody who has more experience being unemployed? I'm very good at it."

It was only then that the full weight of what Tim had done hit Syd. He had sacrificed his job, his stock options, his new-found success. And why?

"This is really amazing," said Syd. "You'd be an excellent spy."

"Actually, I was just being a good reporter. That's what I really want to be. I got a little sidetracked, that's all."

"You should spend the night here. I'll get you a blanket. We can tell your mother everything in the morning."

"Okay," said Tim, emotionally spent. He spread out on the couch.

For the first time in how long—ten years, fifteen?—Syd found himself tucking one of his sons in for the night.

"If you lose your job, you must let me help you," said Syd softly. "You did this for me, and I won't forget it."

"We'll see," said Tim, yawning. "Just think, Dad, I'll be an unemployed writer with a BMW. That's a whole new level of failure for me. I think I should be proud."

## Spinning Plates

**"Okay, so here's my** moral dilemma," said Perry as he and Sandy sat down for dinner at Musso and Frank's. As usual, the restaurant was only partially full—Perry could remember coming here with his family for special occasions, and the wait would be an hour, even if you had a reservation. Plus, once you got seated, you faced the surliest waiters this side of New York. Old and crotchety, they alternately ignored you or made fun of you. Everyone loved Musso's waiters. In a land where every restaurant employed actors in training, the career waiters at Musso's seemed exotic. Perry liked them because he saw too much of himself in the would-be actors and screenwriters who served his food at other eateries. At Musso's, there were no reminders of his career concerns.

"I'm listening," said Sandy.

"I'm being pressured—bribed, almost—to give a kid an *A* who doesn't deserve one. There's the hint of a good job on a TV series if I play ball, and Bob Parrish will clearly be relieved if I give this kid a better grade."

"So what's the problem?" asked Sandy, examining the two thousand items that made up the Musso's menu. "So give him an *A*. What's the big deal?"

"He doesn't deserve an *A*. At best—if he works his butt off—he deserves a *B* or *B*-plus."

"Oh, for Christ's sake," said Sandy, throwing down the menu in exasperation. "It's a grade, not a kidney. Just give it to him. What possible difference will it make in life? Do you even remember the grades you got in high school?"

"No, but I feel guilty being bought, I guess."

"You should only feel guilty if someone is getting hurt. If you had to take an *A* away from a good kid and give it to this loser, then maybe I'd tell you to fight it. But otherwise, what the hell?"

"Did you know most new teachers quit within three years?" asked Perry.

"Makes sense. We both know you're just hiding out at Crosswinds. If you stayed there, you'd eventually be a bitter old guy." As if on cue, a bitter old guy came to take their order. "You'd be like that," said Sandy, motioning to the retreating waiter. "Telling your students about the good old days on game shows."

"Yeah, I guess." Perry sighed.

Perry was starving when his beef Stroganoff came. This meal was a true special occasion, since he, like Ann, rarely allowed himself to eat beef. Sandy had ordered a chef's salad, which was covered with long planks of cheese dripping in dressing. She picked one up with her fingers and took a dainty bite off the end. The weight of the ranch was too great for the cheese, however. It snapped in half and went plummeting toward her lap. Perry's head was down, digging into his meal, but he saw the cheese fall. Sandy, thinking he had missed it, went on eating.

"What about you? Aren't you hiding out at *Hollywood Today*?" Frankly, Perry cared less about that answer and was more intrigued by how long Sandy would pretend that she didn't have a giant piece of cheese in her lap.

"I don't know," she said wistfully. "I had never planned to make a career of it, but I'm having fun. It's been good for me. Painting can be isolating, and it's good for me to be in an office. I met Tim and I met you. That's not bad for one job."

Perry looked directly at her. Sandy was smart, funny, quirky, and vulnerable. He didn't feel as if he was in love with her, but, in a way, that seemed inevitable. If I don't end up falling in love with her, something will be terribly wrong with me, he thought. So he assumed that he was in prelove and acted accordingly.

"I'm glad we met. It's the nicest thing Tim ever did for me."

"Tim, Tim, Tim," said Sandy, shaking her head. "What are we going to do with Tim?"

"I know, he's been a bit much lately," agreed Perry. "That happens. I usually just avoid him until it passes. I don't think I've talked to him since the party last week."

"I've never seen anyone less cut out for success," said Sandy. "Except me."

"The car?"

"The car, the column, that awful Antonio. He should know better."

"Tim hasn't had that much good luck in life," said Perry. "It's not like he's had bad luck, like a car accident or a brain tumor, but things haven't quite gelled. He'll be all over the map with this one—he'll brag, he'll feel unworthy, he'll do something stupid like buy a BMW, but he'll still be Tim. Ultimately, I mean."

"You two are so alike and yet so different."

"That's what everyone says. It's typical of twins, I think. Even we expect our lives to be more in sync than they are. But we've always been totally out of sync. When I'd get a good report card, he'd get a bad one. When things were going well for me socially, he'd be brooding in his room. Mom used to say that she never went to bed unworried—one of us always had a crisis."

"So who's in crisis now? The schoolteacher who's about to be bribed or the hot-shot writer who's making a fool of himself with the TV star boyfriend?"

"I would say it's him. He would say it's me. My mom would worry about both of us."

"I'm more worried about him," offered Sandy. "I think you're luckier."

"Knock on wood when you say that," insisted Perry, instinctively reaching under the table and knocking on the wooden underside. Sandy knocked on the side of her chair.

"Can I tell you something without hurting your feelings?" asked Perry. "Actually, can I tell you two things?"

"You can try."

"You're the first girl I've dated since high school I didn't want to form a production company with. I mean that in the best possible way. I never thought that I could have a relationship that wasn't centered on work. I was afraid that I'd have nothing to talk about. But it's different with you, different in a very good way."

"Okay, that wasn't so bad," said Sandy. "What's number two?"

"I know you have a big piece of cheese in your lap. But I'm

going to the men's room so that you can take care of it with a minimum of humiliation." He stood up and headed for the back of the restaurant.

"Perry?" Sandy called out after him.

He turned back.

"I hate you," she said sweetly.

"I know," he said. "I don't blame you."

# One Instant Message Too Many

**Tim was usually not** a stupid man, but it took three unreturned phone calls to Antonio before he became suspicious. At first, he wrote it off to Antonio's hectic filming schedule, or his rigorous daily meetings with his high-priced personal trainer. ("You should meet him," he'd once told Tim. "It's the best two hundred dollars a week you could spend.") But three calls and four days had passed, and there was no word from the best-looking boyfriend Tim had ever had.

It was 10:00 P.M., and even Antonio would be home by now, thought Tim. He placed one more phone call, feeling super-pathetic and needy. Once again, he got voice mail.

Lacking anything better to do, Tim went on-line. There, in his buddy list, along with two coworkers, one old high school friend, and his mother, was Star77777, the self-aggrandizing screen name Antonio had adopted.

> **TimTimTim:** I just called you.
> **Star77777:** Sorry, I've been very busy.
> **TimTimTim:** Maybe we should talk.
> **PandTMom:** Hi, Tim!

Perfect. Ann was now interrupting his instant messages, as well.

> **TimTimTim:** Hi, Mom. How's life?
> **PandTMom:** You've made your father very happy. He keeps telling everyone how brave you are.
> **TimTimTim:** Glad to be of service. Has he talked to any of the partners yet?
> **Star77777:** I know. I've been putting this off for too long.
> **TimTimTim:** If I call, will you answer?
> **Star77777:** Let me call you. It's better that way.
> **TimTimTim:** Why can't I call you?
> **Star77777:** I don't want you to.
> **TimTimTim:** You don't want me to call now? Or ever?
> **Star77777:** I'll call you. Just wait.
> **PandTMom:** He's already shown the papers to two partners and now they're scared to death of the new deal. You're a hero.
> **TimTimTim:** I don't understand, Antonio. I thought we were having a relationship. It certainly seemed like a relationship. I have three shirts of yours hanging in my closet right now. But I CAN'T CALL YOU!!!! Why?

There are drawbacks to juggling too many IMs, and Tim ran headlong into the worst of them. As soon as he clicked the send button, he realized that the message meant for Antonio had gone to his mother instead. It was more than an instant message. It was an instant outing.

Tim stared at his screen. His mind scrambled to think of any excuse to tell his mother. He reread the message he had sent, looking for wiggle room. Why did he have to mention the shirts? Why didn't he own a gun? Blowing his brains out seemed like such a viable option at the moment.

The screen seemed inactive for much too long. He thought about signing off, leaving town, maybe throwing the computer down a flight of steps. Then he heard the familiar IM tone that sounds like Tinker Bell spreading pixie dust.

> **PandTMom:** If Antonio treats you like that, he's an ass-hole. You deserve much better.

Sandy would be proud, thought Tim. I've finally come out to my parents. Who would have thought it would have happened this way!

> **TimTimTim:** Thanks, Mom. It's a tough time. I feel like my life is unraveling. I'm going to sign off now before I get in more trouble.
>
> **PandTMom:** You're not in any trouble. We love you. Call me.
>
> **TimTimTim:** I will. Bye.

Tim was still feeling shell-shocked when the phone rang. Antonio was so cold and distant, it was hard to believe that they had ever been friends, let alone lovers. Antonio's stock excuses ran together in Tim's already-overloaded brain. "Not working out/This isn't what I want/Too many differences/Now's a bad time for a relationship."

"Fine," said Tim defiantly. "I don't care. It's over. I get it. I'm amazed it ever happened. I'll drop off your shirts when you're not there. Have a nice life."

But Antonio wasn't done. "And that hair story you wrote—what were you thinking?"

"What does that have to with any of this?" asked Tim. "It's just a story."

"You just don't get it, do you?" said an angry Antonio. "You were making fun of some very important people. Why would you make fun of Brian Grazer? What has he ever done to you?"

"He didn't do anything. He just has very silly hair. He's a big boy. He can take it."

"I'm disappointed in you. I thought you wanted something better. But you're stuck in your little world and you refuse to see that there's a bigger, better world. But you insist on staying on your stupid little planet."

"Antonio, I don't have a clue what you're talking about and I'm not even sure I care," said Tim.

"Exactly," replied Antonio triumphantly. "That's what I'm trying to tell you. You don't get it. Do you know why you don't get it? My friends were right: Journalists are just a bunch of losers."

"So I've been told," said Tim. "It seems to be the theme for this week."

# Negotiation for Dummies

**Rubin Carson's office on** the Paramount lot was, like most studio offices, more functional than elegant. Yet it still reeked of power—how many unimportant men needed three full-time executive assistants to manage the traffic and correspondence flow?

It was one of the three middle-aged women—Perry had no idea which one—who had sent for Perry. The call was matter-of-fact: "Mr. Newman, this is Linda Feidelson from Mr. Carson's office. He'd like to see you Friday at four-fifteen sharp. I'll leave a drive on for you at the gate. Oh, and Mr. Carson has a very busy schedule that day. You might want to arrive a few minutes early, just to be on the safe side."

Safety first, thought Perry, who was safely seated in the

reception area at 3:45. Not that he expected Rubin Carson to be on time, but he was Rubin Carson—he was allowed to be late. Perry was Perry Newman. He was supposed to be on time.

So it was no surprise that Rubin was late. Exactly one hour and five minutes late. Unforgivable in any businesses except show business and medicine.

"Come in, come in," said Rubin finally, moving behind his large desk in front of the big window that overlooked the unglamorous Paramount parking lot. He offered no apologies. He didn't have to.

"Alex tells me that everything is working out fine," said Rubin. "I like that. It makes me happy."

"He's a good kid. I think we found a way for everyone to be happy."

"He tells me you're a good teacher. Why would you want to quit something you're good at?"

Uh-oh, here it comes, thought Perry. The big letdown.

"I'm glad he thinks I'm a good teacher," said Perry with a certain steely determination. "And I've enjoyed it as a change of pace. But I'm only twenty-six years old—I need to build a career I can live with, doing what I really want to do. Maybe someday, years from now, I'll go back to teaching. Right now, though, I have a life to think about."

"I read your pilot," said Rubin, waving the script in the air. "Boy, did you get screwed on that one."

Carson does his homework, thought Perry. Perry had ruled out sending the script, thinking it was too blatant a job pitch. Carson had clearly gotten one on his own—or had had one of the three women out front do it.

"I think I told you at school—it was a bad experience on several levels."

"And yet you're willing to try again."

Perry laughed. "How much worse can it get?"

Rubin laughed, too. "I'm going to give you a job, you know."

"I'm very glad to hear that."

"But it's not a great job. Do you know why?"

"First off, I'm grateful for any job. I know I don't have a big track record yet. I've worked on one cable game show and one pilot I was fired from. I understand I'm still a rookie in your eyes."

Rubin shook his head. "That's not why. I'll tell you why. You were too easy. A smart person would have put up more of struggle and made me work to get Alex that *A*. You bent over like Liberace in the shower room. You should have made me sweat. You had the power. Crosswinds could have gotten another half mil for bleachers in the gymnasium. But no—you just said, 'Yes, Mr. Carson, sir.' I'm telling you this because I have faith in you. But if you're going to make it, you have to toughen up. This is hardball. Understand?"

"I think so," said Perry, adding cagily, "I might have been blinded by my genuine affection for Alex. I wanted him to do well."

"Nice try. I like that. That comeback gets an *A* for effort. But it's too little too late. But you're smart. You'll learn." He shook his head. "Genuine affection for Alex. Sheesh.

"I have seven shows on the air right now. Despite that bravura comeback, you're starting at the bottom. Well, the bottom of my shows. It's certainly a hell of a step up from a game show."

"Can I ask which show it is?"

"That syndicated one that plays at four A.M., *when* I'm lucky. The one with the Playboy Playmate, where she plays an undercover officer on a college campus. *Sorority Cop.* You'll be a staff writer. You'll start as soon as school is out—which is what, another month? We'll save your slot. You'll get Writers' Guild scale, and Perry—"

"Yes."

"If you're not running the show by the end of the season, I'll be very disappointed. I've got turkeys running it now and I want them out. You can help me."

Perry nodded.

"Linda will take you over to the offices. They're expecting you. And Perry, if Linda smokes on the walk over, grab the cigarette out of her mouth and crush it. Do you hear me? That woman smokes like a Pittsburgh steel mill, and I want her to stop. She's going to die at her desk out there, and it'll just distract everybody. It's driving me crazy."

"Will do, sir," said Perry, giving Rubin a joke salute.

"It's been a pleasure doing business with you," said Rubin. "Be creative, but be ruthless, too."

"I'll try," said Perry.

A few steps out of the building and Linda lit a Virginia Slim.

"I'm under strict orders not to let you smoke," said Perry. "Rubin said I should yank that cigarette right out of your mouth."

Linda looked Perry square in the eye. "Fuck him," she said, and took another drag.

## Tim Gets Fired—While Sleeping

**Dumped by his boyfriend,** outed to his parents, and about to lose his job, Tim did what depressed people did in the days before Celexa: He slept. Not ten hours. Not twelve. He stayed in bed, half-sleeping, half-staring at the ceiling, for a day and a half. The phone would ring occasionally, but he ignored all calls, not even listening to the messages. He did make one exception—a call from his mother. It was in Ann's nature to expect something melodramatic, so he took her call, just to reassure her that he hadn't committed suicide. He chose his tenses carefully. He didn't say he "wouldn't," only that he "hadn't."

Finally, he decided to get up, if only because he had started to smell funny. It was 10:00 A.M. on Friday, and he supposed he should show up for work. He was entitled, he figured, to some sort of severance; plus, it would be nice to have that Rolodex here at home while he tried freelancing.

Having showered but still carrying an odd odor, he walked to his BMW—imagining the FOR SALE signs he'd soon be placing in the rear windows. He drove slowly to work. He was in no rush to see Simon.

The office was much more active than usual when he walked in. Everyone was scurrying about, chattering loudly, carrying boxes. It was almost like an office party.

"Congratulations," said Sandy, handing him a box. "You just managed to sleep through getting fired."

His brain was still foggy. He knew why *he* had a box, but he wasn't sure why everyone else had them, too. Why, for instance, was Sandy packing her belongings?

"We've all been let go," she said. "As of midnight last night, *Hollywood Today* ceased to exist. Synergistic pulled the plug on us. We had a big meeting; they told us we were a noble experiment but that there were too many other sites like us on the Web. They've decided to concentrate their resources elsewhere."

"You're fucking kidding," said Tim.

"Nope, Simon made a beautiful speech and then he cried. He said he had been a fool, that Synergistic had planned to close us down months ago and he just didn't see the signs. He felt that he'd led us all astray. But he told us we should all stay in touch—that journalism is a network of friends, and that he'd do his best to help us all find jobs. And then he left. Look—his office is totally barren."

Indeed it was, as if it had never been occupied at all.

She handed Tim an envelope marked "Confidential." He opened it.

---

*Dear Tim,*

*By the time you read this, I will have apologized to the entire staff for encouraging them to believe in what turned out to be a house of cards. I was greedy, and in my greed, I allowed myself to be stupid, not seeing the warning signs someone of my experience should know all too well.*

*I owe you an even bigger apology. You were the best, and yet I allowed you to see me at my worst. We're all complicated and conflicted humans, and while I can't deny that the immoral, greedy side I showed you the other day exists, I'd like to think that the other Simon James, the one who loved his work and appreciated talent such as yours, existed, as well. For years, good Simon won out over bad Simon. You saw the one skirmish where good Simon was annihilated.*

*Forgive me. I know that you gave some valuable documents to your father, and for that, I thank you. It taught me something. You're never too old to learn, me included.*

*I can't do much for you, but I have done this.* Hollywood Today *may be dead, but your syndication deal lives on. I phoned Arthur in New York this morning and got his assurance that you could continue doing your column for all your papers. You'll still have an income, and while it's about half what you're used to, you're no worse off than when you started here. Call Arthur early next week and work out the details.*

*I'm sorry and thanks. I think that says it all.*

Tim folded the letter and put it in his shirt pocket.

"Do we still have E-mail?" he asked Sandy.

"Just for today, so you better check it."

Tim signed on and found yet another E-mail from Mom.

> *Dear Tim,*
>
> *Your father must have called you twenty times last night. He heard they were closing your company down and he wanted to tell you. He feels so bad, he can't even enjoy his own good news—the partners decided not to sell. Please call your dad. He's worried sick. (So am I, but I'm always worried.)*
>
> *Love,*
> *Mom*

"Now what?" asked Tim.

"I already have a job interview next week," said Sandy. "Simon set it up. An on-line art dealer. I'd write catalog copy. That might be more up my alley anyway, if I get it. What about you?"

"I get to keep the newspaper column," he said. "And other than that, I think I'm making a fresh start."

"Antonio?"

"Gone. Ancient history. Ancient *rude* history."

"I'm sorry to hear that."

"No you're not, but thanks for lying." Tim smiled. "And I came out to Mom and Dad. Accidentally, but it's done."

"You're having a big week, aren't you?"

"It seems that way. I liked life so much better last week."

"Maybe," said Sandy. "Maybe you didn't. It wasn't a very Tim life, I don't think. In a lot of ways, you seemed happier when I first met you."

Tim wasn't sure she was entirely wrong. His new life hadn't

fit well, but he'd assumed he'd grow into it. Now he'd never know.

"So, do you know anybody stupid enough to want to buy my BMW?" Tim asked.

Sandy thought about it for a moment. "Well, there's Perry. He's dumb in almost the same way you are."

## Ann Performs a Miracle—Or Not

**Tim and Perry arrived** in the driveway for Sunday dinner at almost exactly the same time.

"How's my old car?" asked Tim, looking somewhat mournfully at the BMW that had once been his.

"It's not exactly the fastest car in the world," said Perry. "But it'll do. At least when I get to the Paramount lot, I'll have a BMW. Maybe not the best BMW, but it's a BMW, and that counts for something."

"Didn't you forget something?" asked Tim as they head toward the front door.

Perry looked at Tim's empty hands, then down at his own.

"Whose turn was it to bring dinner?" asked Perry. "Mom never said anything to me."

"Me, neither. Do you think she forgot?"

"If she did, she'll just send one of us out for it."

Once in the house, though, it was clear that this was not going to be any ordinary dinner. For one thing, the house smelled as if someone was cooking. For another, Ann was nowhere to be seen.

"Where's Mom," asked Perry as he and Tim entered the den. Syd, sitting in his comfortable chair, was watching *Entertainment Tonight*'s weekend wrap-up show.

Syd put his finger to his lips and spoke in a soft whisper. "I don't know how to tell you this, boys, but your mother is in the kitchen. She's cooking dinner."

"I didn't know Mom knew where the kitchen was," marveled Tim.

"I should have brought a camera," said Perry. "Sandy will never believe this."

"I'm in a state of shock myself," said Syd. "She downloaded recipes from the Internet. Frankly, I'm frightened."

"Hey, Mom, we're here!" yelled Perry.

"Stay where you are," answered Ann, raising her voice to be heard over the sound of a Cuisinart operating on the pulse mode.

"Don't hurt yourself," shouted Tim.

Tim sat down, while Perry rummaged through the wet bar looking for a diet Coke.

"What are we watching?" asked Perry.

"Famous people at a premiere, I guess," said Syd.

"Oh, look, Tim, it's Kato Kaelin," said Perry impishly. Tim turned a slight shade of red. Fortunately, luck was with him.

"And isn't that the star of the very show that just hired you?" he asked as a busty, Naughahyde-clad beauty paused for the cameras.

"I want everyone to know that this is genuine artificial

leather," she told the camera. "I'm a member of PETA and I don't think any animal should suffer for my happiness."

"She's actually not all that bad," said Perry defensively. "I hear she shows up on time and she knows her lines."

Syd stood. "I'll check on your mother," he said, and wandered off to the kitchen. His timing had never been better. Tim and Perry sat in slack-jawed amazement as the next celebrity couple wandered down the red carpet. No couple could have been more shocking, more bizarre, more overwhelming, more unexpected than what Tim and Perry saw.

"Tell me I'm hallucinating," said Perry.

"This is like a bad dream," agreed Tim.

The host gushed as WB hunk Antonio Lopez approached the camera with his newest girlfriend.

"Antonio, please introduce us to your date," urged Jann Carl.

"Thanks, Jann. This is my fiancée, Nancy Marshall. She's the writer-producer behind *Dire Straights* on NBC."

"You must be very happy," gushed Jann. "That show's a gigantic hit."

"What are the odds that your ex and my ex would end up engaged?" asked Perry.

"This is even weirder than Mom cooking," said Tim.

"It doesn't matter. I've lost my appetite," complained Perry.

It took a few seconds, but finally both boys burst out laughing, laughing so hard that tears rolled down their cheeks, neither could stand up straight, and neither one of them could stop.

Through the haze of tears, they looked up and saw a confused set of parents standing over them.

"What in the hell has gotten into you two?" asked Syd.

Through gasps of air, Perry tried to explain, but he couldn't.

"It was something on TV," Tim said, "but you had to see it. It was just so funny."

And at that, they started laughing again. They were still laughing as they sat down at the dinner table and began their salad.

"I know everyone has been through a lot of excitement the past few months," said Ann, serving—actually *serving*—helpings of salad to her family, "but I have an announcement of my own."

Tim and Perry instinctively looked away from each other, so as not to encourage reactive laughter.

"As you know, I've been having a wonderful time with my yoga lessons, and I don't think I'm sounding conceited if I tell you that my teacher thinks I have a real talent for yoga. She's asked me to get involved in a very special program that I think will mean a lot to me. I'm going to learn to teach yoga, but I won't be just some ordinary yoga teacher here in the Valley. This program is brand-new, and it has some exciting people involved with it. Once I'm trained, I'll be part of a very select group that will travel all over Los Angeles teaching yoga to the people who need it most—the homeless."

Tim dug his thumbnail into his arm, trying to inflict enough pain to prevent the giggles. Perry, on the other hand, bit his lower lip so severely that he could taste blood.

Only Syd was brave enough to answer. "I think that's wonderful, dear," he said with a perfectly straight face. "That's just what the homeless need."

"Why, thank you," said Ann, and she returned to her home-cooked feast, a variety of dishes she had found on various Web sites and then had printed out and spent the day preparing. Even though these were complicated recipes, she'd actually enjoyed the whole process. Of course, that practically guaranteed that her meal would be perfect: the vichyssoise (a first for her; she'd never even eaten it in a restaurant, let alone prepared it), the mint-flavored pasta (another first!), the blue corn with pine nuts, the homemade rosemary bread, the chicken with black butter and fennel—and just wait until the Newman men got to dessert, a mouthwatering sour cherry clafouti. And to think that she hadn't really cooked a big meal in years. That's one of the wonderful things about the Internet, she thought, how it awakens old passions in you that you thought were long dead.

Everyone ate and ate, raving about the once-in-a-lifetime experience. Perry talked about his new show and Sandy. Tim was proud of some changes he was making in his syndicated column. Syd was quiet, but he was a happy man—Newman's Super Honda had been saved and the family was once again together on a Sunday night. Ann was totally thrilled; she beamed as plate after plate returned to the kitchen empty.

Later, as Ann tidied up the kitchen, Syd, Perry, and Tim, ashen and queasy, took refuge in the privacy of the den and agreed it was the worst meal they had ever eaten.

# acknowledgments

**For help at various stages** along the way (in my life, or maybe just this book), I'd like to thank my parents, my brother Mark, the Greenfield family, Jim Morgan, Kathy Robbins, Peter Sikowitz, Michael Parrish, David Strick, Arthur Kretchmer, Linda Feidelson, Alice Turner, Jonathan Black, John Rezek, Chris Napolitano, Lee Froehlich, Kevin Buckley, David Sheff, Cindy Rakowitz, Michael Sigman, Lew Harris, Geoff Miller, Susan Squire, Jim Nagle, Joe Saltzman, Jack Langguth, Herb Chase, Kassie Evashevski, the late Judy Sims and the real Rubin Carson.

**I'd also like to thank** my excellent agent and friend, Bill Clegg, my supportive and smart editor, Elizabeth Beier, and most of all Sue Horton, who can see things others (especially me) cannot.